The Family of Chosen

Foundation of Kings

Raymond L. Mungro Jr.

iUniverse, Inc.
Bloomington

iUniverse books may be ordered through booksellers or by contacting:

iUniverse
1663 Liberty Drive
Bloomington, IN 47403
www.iuniverse.com
1-800-Authors (1-800-288-4677)

ISBN: 978-1-4502-9889-6 (sc)
ISBN: 978-1-4502-9890-2 (ebook)

Printed in the United States of America

iUniverse rev. date: 02/22/2011

Acknowledgements

I would like to give thanks to God for inspiring and enabling me to tell a tale of this magnitude. I would also like to thank everyone that assisted me with giving the public this story; Tanakia Harris, the Harris Family, the entire Mungro family and friends. Your input and insight helped me to place my thoughts on paper. I hope you enjoy reading the story as much as I enjoyed writing it for you.

Prologue

Washington D.C. 2008 A.D.

The rumble of the subway train on this trip seems exceptionally loud. Perhaps it is because I believe that I am being followed and I want to hear every conversation and see anyone moving around me. The Metro doors chime (ding dong, doors closing) I focus on everyone in an attempt to see if any one was going out of their way not to stare at me. Any one of them may be the person or persons following me. It is always hard to tell if you are being followed, but if you pay close enough attention you can spot them. The Conductor's voice came on over the loudspeaker, "Your next stop, Ronald Reagan National Airport, doors will open on the left." I take a second to ponder whether I should walk now or wait until the last moment and run out. I had decided on the latter. The train pulled into the station and I positioned myself close enough to the exit as to be able to jump out before they were closed.

The doors opened and I stood aside as people boarded. The Metro doors started to chime and close. I leapt from the train so no one would follow. I felt silly as I almost lost my balance but these precautions are necessary at a time like this. I had reached a moment in my life where current events intersected with my dreams of the kingdoms of old. Things are finally starting to make sense and I would not be stopped so far into my journey. I had travelled so far to get here, seems to have been through space and time itself. The flight to New York connecting me to Israel, the Israel of my time departed in an hour. I passed through security and boarded my flight early without encountering any unforeseen incidents. I did not know exactly which government agency had me followed but I expected to be delayed attempting to board a plane leaving the country and the ease in which I boarded surprised me.

I sat in my seat and gazed out of the window at the Control Tower as if waiting for the tower to send word to stop my plane. I sighed deeply and reflected on how everything started, if I am not mistaken I believe on my thirteenth birthday the first visit occurred. I thought harder about the subject and shook my head in agreement with myself because my birthday seemed to be when this marvelous voyage began. My mind transported me twenty years in the past.

Philadelphia 1980 A.D.

I flipped through a National Geographic Magazine for my eighth grade teacher Ms. McDermott's homework assignment. I remembered reading in some cultures I would have already been considered a man at the age of thirteen. I thought to myself how wonderful it would be if I were in ancient Egypt. I probably would be able to be Pharaoh at thirteen. My mom begged to differ as she beckoned for me to take out the trash. I rose off of my unmade bottom bunk and ran down the stairs towards my mother who screamed for me from the kitchen. I started to wonder where my family came from. My Grandfather told stories of our royalty and of the blessed men of the family. I thought every family in America believed their family special and we all are ancestors of African Kings. The Black Pride, back to Africa movement consistently echoed this fact. To my surprise I would soon learn otherwise.

I grabbed the two trash bags from the kitchen and walked through the dining room towards the living room and to the front door. I pondered who I was and what my destiny was? I burned for knowledge and needed questions to be answered. I said my prayers as I did every other night except for one favor. I asked the Lord to *show me the history of my family and to help me determine my destiny*. I didn't want my life to be useless. I wanted purpose. My thirteen year old mind raced whilst I lay in my bottom bunk making it difficult to fall asleep, until everything went black and sleep finally overcame me, well I thought it was sleep anyway.

Chapter One: The Road to Jerusalem

1003 B.C.

I awoke the next morning under a cloudless blue sky riding alongside a tall man with a stern bearded handsome face. He reminded me of my Grandfather. Startled a bit because of my surroundings, I rationalized that I must still be dreaming.

My voice trembling I asked him, "Sir, who are you, to where do we ride and what land am I in?"

The tall man glanced down at me as if he knew who I was and answered, "You are a guest of the Kings from the Lord. I am to show you what you seek. In the following years you will spend time in my families' presence. Welcome Mustafa."

I interjected, "Please call me Moosie." I hated my full name so much I usually responded in almost a reflex reaction to hearing it. I then stuttered, "Wait, did, did you say years?"

The armor clad man continued, "Mustafa, I am King David and we are marching to take Jerusalem."

I blinked shielding my eyes from the hot sun and muttered, "We?" I thought to myself how the King must not have understood when I said call me Moosie or maybe he is too royal or something for nicknames. He smiled then nodded his head as if to tell me to turn around. Behind me was a grand army. Somehow, I now rode with King David as he moved to capture Jerusalem. My heart almost leapt from my chest at the vividness of this dream. His tarnished heavy brass Chariot pulled by his two battle hardened white chariot horses sped along the sandy, stone and pebble-covered terrain found along the paths towards Jerusalem. I gazed at the Golden Star emblem emblazoned over the sky blue background of his battle standard and began to rub my eyes, "Was I dreaming." I was just lying in my bunk a minute ago in Twentieth Century Philadelphia. I mean I was thirteen for goodness sake.

Just then King David began to pray aloud, "This battle Lord, this great campaign I am about to undertake, I beseech you to bless. If it is your will that Jerusalem is to be my city, it will be your city as well and my family will forever honor you there as your servants for all of time. I will build a grand city in which to praise you and show all how glorious you are." He then turned to me and said, "Mustafa, you will bear witness to my covenant with the Lord and know as I do that failure to take Jerusalem will be my families' end." He explained how he could not suffer failure; years of warfare for and against King Saul had enabled him to make major diplomatic moves in the region in preparation for him to architect a siege of this magnitude. Silently moving behind David and I under the warmth of the day's sun on our way to the fate awaiting us in Jerusalem was a massive army of one hundred thousand Chariots, one hundred thousand Horsemen and two hundred thousand Infantry men. There were men marching for miles behind us.

As we rode onward to Jerusalem David seemed to notice my fright and uneasiness. I was a child far from home and marching into a warzone.

As if reading my mind he told me, "Mustafa there is no need to worry. As long as I have breath in my body you will never be harmed during your stay with my family."

I believed his words. He said, "The Assyrians, Philistines, Moabites and Edomites all follow clumsily to record the events of this day closely."

He pointed at the mountains and I barely made out the figures of men running to and fro in the shadows. There were spies following behind his splendid army far enough away as to not interfere with the advance. They constantly sent runners back and forth informing their Kings the Twelve Tribes of Judah were on the move, and the King himself led the attack.

David smiled as he spread his arms toward the army and said, "Mustafa these forces were hired and paid for solely by me for this purpose. A force made entirely of mercenaries and conscripts from all over. The twelve tribes of Judah remain behind safely in their homes watching and waiting for any news as I move on to secure Jerusalem as my Capital. There are a few members of the tribes here though serving as commanders. I handpicked most but some have volunteered to travel with us for the glory of fighting for their King. Truces have been arranged so Hebron would remain safe during my absence, but if I am defeated in battle any truce in place would not prevent a King from helping himself to the spoils of Hebron."

"Our final strategy is simple, attack the impregnable garrison from the Valley of Hinnom and assault the wall above Herod's Palace with hordes of men. By attacking the shortest area of the wall with massive numbers, King Herod would not be able to place enough soldiers to stop a full onslaught. We will overrun the Corner Gate like a wave over a beach."

For the remainder of the trip David remained silent as if deep in thought. Later that evening as we camped he introduced me to his nephew and able captain of the host, Joab.

Joab spoke with a low but calming voice, "We would bring a child to this battlefield?"

David quickly answered, "He is no mere child, and he will be our guest here for awhile. He is given full access of the kingdom and full access to the King and his safety is as paramount as mine."

Joab grunted, "Well then boy, welcome to the siege of Jerusalem."

He was the rough brutish type you would not wish to be alone in a room with, but just the type you would want on your side in a fight. David's plan of attack did not sit well with Joab, and he wasted no time letting David know. Joab began his report to David, "My King, we will suffer enormous casualties, but the massive strike should make way for a much faster victory. I am also concerned about Hebron's defense and do not wish to engage the entire force. I would demand that several companies of chariots and a contingent of infantry remain fresh in the rear in order to dash back to Hebron in the case of an attack there."

David promptly agreed with his captain, "Joab, once again you are correct. I would prefer for these reserves to be left out of the fray. Carry on with your plans; we have to ensure our attack is over within two days time. We do not want the city to reinforce itself."

Joab nodded in approval as to confer with David's fears and answered, "A siege would prove most disastrous for our offensive. You are absolutely right this conquest must be done as quickly and humanely as possible."

David turned to me and said, "Jerusalem is the center of trade in the region and for its citizens to be under siege or abused might foster pity from those neighboring kingdoms who would start to lose income from a lack of trade with Jerusalem and they may decide to move against us. We cannot permit this to happen."

Joab then informed David of his plans for the chariots, "I am keeping a company of chariots on the surrounding roads to stop all traffic from entering the city. They are instructed to permit women, children and noncombatants to leave. This will also keep the chariots from battle and will allow them to rest in case they had to gallop back to Hebron in its defense. Upon reaching the outskirts of the valley and Jerusalem's walls we should allow the men the afternoon and late into the evening to rest after our long march. Later in the night I shall move the troops within the Valley of Hinnom and position them around the wall to set up for the ensuing mornings attack."

David agreed with Joab's plans and they were set into motion. Jerusalem got considerably cool which felt sort of strange to me because did one usually feel cold in a dream? Everything around me was so vivid? Clouds had also moved over the battlefield making the sparsely vegetated and barren terrain much darker, so Joab ordered the cavalry to set up campfires off into the distant south and to the distant north of the city in order to confuse the tower guards of the direction in which to prepare the wall for the next day's attack.

"Hopefully, the surprise of an attack at dawn will give us the edge and the time we need for a quick victory. Good night Joab, may the Lord bless you in battle on the morn." David said as the two warriors hugged each other.

"As may he bless you David, good night." Joab replied as he left David's tent.

The night passed slowly, but hardly anyone including David slept. I felt nervous as well. I did not know what the morning had in store for King David but wanted desperately to wake up before the battle began. I was surprised I had not already awakened because this dream was getting a little too scary for me and I usually wake myself from a dream before anything got out of hand. I held myself from crying as I thought how far from Philadelphia I was and how I missed my family. I wiped my tears and thought I couldn't be the boy I was at home in this new place. It was time for me to grow up and stop being scared of everything. The harsh streets of North Philly were no war zone but I was sure anything this dream threw at me would be nothing compared to the bully and gang infested walk to and from school.

I walked from my tent to take in some of the night air and found David outside as well. He seemed startled as he turned around. I sat silently by the fire taking in my surroundings.

He sat next to me and said, "Before a battle like the one we will be in tomorrow a man must spend his possible last hours on this earth reflecting on his life and asking forgiveness for prior sins." He sighed then continued, "If I should meet my fate on tomorrow's battlefield what would happen to my family? Would they be safe, how would my death affect my children?" He stood up and turned towards the glorious stone walls of Jerusalem.

He mumbled so I could barely hear him, "The walls of Jerusalem are the best constructed walls I have ever seen. The city is so beautiful." He switched the conversation to lighter subjects.

I looked upon the Walls of Jerusalem and stood in awe. The masonry was exquisite for the time. Each huge stone was as if it were prepared and imported from some far off land and hand placed. There were no edges in which one could climb or hide under. Behind this huge wall that stretched for miles in a rectangular shape was Jerusalem, a large bustling city with over three hundred thousand people. I thought to myself this was not bad for 1000 BC. The attack David was commanding and I was about to bare witness to was monumental. David could in one day have enough gold and wealth to sustain his kingdom throughout his lifetime with the successful invasion of this wealthy trade center. I knew David wanted desperately to take the city as he talked of how those walls would soon be his.

He sat back down and bit into a peach as he spoke, "I would love to build Jerusalem to be the greatest city the world has ever known. A beautiful strategically placed capital that could never be rivaled or conquered. Tomorrow's battle is my first step to achieving this empire. This battle will be a mighty undertaking, win or lose it will never be taken lightly and will always be remembered throughout time." He stood up from the stool yawned then turned to me and said, "Goodnight Mustafa, sleep well tomorrow will be a long day." David walked into his tent and closed the flap behind him.

As the first light bent over the horizon and reflected off the walls of Jerusalem, I was awakened by a tremendous sound. At first I smiled because I thought for a moment I was back at home and was being serenaded by the sounds of the city. Then I opened my eyes only to realize I was still held captive in this realistic dream. I ran from my tent to find out what the tremendous noise had been. David had ordered for all the horns of the host to be sounded. The noise was so loud it cracked the walls of Jerusalem in places.

I heard women screaming in the distance while the children began to cry aloud for their fathers who were scurrying to and fro in order to defend the walls. Only the bravest of men in Jerusalem did not wish to break and run. The ground shook and David's mighty army sent Jerusalem into panic, everyone in the city readied for the attack, shops closed while mothers ran and grabbed their children who had begun gathering in the streets. King Herod ordered all gates to be sealed locked and defended to the death. As the horns halted, David sent Joab to the large bronze gate to ask for the city's immediate surrender. Joab rode off on his horse towards the forty foot high and heavily guarded gate doors.

6

David smiled and whispered to me, "I am glad Joab is with me on this day. He is respected by the entire army and is the leader of my personal guard the "Thirty". He is a phenomenal commander and has many battle scars to go with the stories he loves to tell everyone about how he got them."

Around the camp many men talked of Joab. He was seven years David's senior and he was supposedly as sharp a tactician as any David had ever faced. During my short time with them I discovered Joab was often times soft-spoken with family and friends. The men talked of his ruthlessness in battle which was an exact opposite to the soft-spoken demeanor displayed. He was now riding towards Jerusalem's gates to an uncertain doom. He refused to wear a war helmet, he wanted the enemy to look upon his face and to "see his determination to kill" as he would put it.

His blue commander's cape flew behind him in the wind as he galloped ferociously towards Jerusalem's gate, oblivious to the horns sounding in the distance. His eyes seemed to stay focused on a fixed point right above the gates where the tower guards scurried here and there with anxiety as they prepared for the oncoming invasion. His aides and flag bearer struggled to keep up with his furious pace as they rode displaying the Star of David to the large heavily guarded gates of Jerusalem.

Joab yelled to the tower guards, "Throw down your weapons and welcome the new King into Jerusalem, or would you rather deal with what you see standing before you and he in which you do not see above you."

The tower guard sneered back, "Your King will never be welcomed here. He will never enter these walls. The blind and lame will help to turn him from this city. He will die on this battlefield in front of these mighty walls just as all of our other enemies have done before him. Be gone Hebrew find another city to sack."

Joab rode back to King David and told him of the remarks. David's eyes set ablaze. The tower guard's seemed to infuriate him. He threw the map he was looking at to the ground and stood high upon his chariot, his battle leather tightened and helmet secured David yelled so the whole of his words were heard throughout the ranks as tears of anticipation ran down his dusty face, "Scale these walls and take Jerusalem. They mock your army as we cover the valley and they mock this King brought forth to take their city. They mock my Lord who will deliver Jerusalem unto me this day. Every man here will be remembered forever in history. Take these walls, and let us feast in the city of Jerusalem tonight. There will be no lame or blind left in Jerusalem this day, for this day I hate the lame and the blind so let each blow be to the windpipe for the House of David."

David then grabbed his ivory war horn from the belt around his waist and blew a loud thunderous note triggering an orchestra of war horns that sent a chill up every spine as the infantry poured across the valley towards the gates of Jerusalem screaming ***"For the House of David"***, so began the battle for Jerusalem.

Chapter Two: Assault on Jerusalem

As the infantry rushed Jerusalem's outer walls, a company of archers lined up within range of Jerusalem in four long rows to fire from the front of the Gate of Gennal. The first row shot fire arrows over the wall to create havoc behind the tower. With every order he explained to me the reason for the order, as if I were his war pupil. David looked upon the walls of Jerusalem as he said, "Young Mustafa the fires burning will guarantee the enemy will have to invest soldiers into putting out those fires. The manpower spent putting them out is the manpower not firing at my troops from atop the wall."

The last three rows of archers took turns firing giving the charging hoards of David's infantry and the first row of his archers the cover they needed in order to complete the charge to the walls. The enemy archers were effectively pinned down. They showered Herod's forces with a continuous barrage of arrows allowing the infantry to set up ladders against Jerusalem's outer stone wall. The archers hit Jerusalem with great effectiveness but the tower guard fought gallantly in defense of their city. Many ladders were destroyed by pouring oil down them and lighting the wood on fire as men climbed up. One company managed to breach the tower; they took many casualties and continued to fight bravely.

My gaze went back to David as he sprung into action to reinforce this company of men. David sprang from the Chariot and called frantically for his cavalry horse. His face became stern and hard, with a cold seriousness in his voice he said to me, "Mustafa, stay with my chariot, you will be safe here." He ran and jumped for the stirrups as he saddled his horse in mid gallop racing towards the battle. As he galloped towards the wall he barked commands to the infantry captains he passed along the way pointing to the locations in which he wanted them to attack. His presence seemed to motivate the men and inject them with courage. It even inspired me to peek from the bottom of the chariot at the King moving towards the battle followed by his ever present and fearless guard the "Thirty" dressed in their black capes and gold war helmets.

From my hiding place within the chariot I saw the whole battle unfold. David, galloping on horseback, aimed his bow and fired four arrow shots into the chests of four guards firing on his men from the tower directly above. Those who witnessed the four arrow shots from David with their own eyes looked upon the amazing and legendary accuracy of their King first hand. These shots allowed three ladders to be placed. His personal guard climbed to the top and breached the tower. Directly over the gate where earlier the guards had mocked him had been cleared of enemies but not secured and David wanted desperately to secure it. King Herod's soldiers began a counter attack so David had to act quickly. The first row of archers continued shooting fire arrows into the city creating the chaos David needed to get the time for the "Thirty" to open the gate for Joab's forces.

Once opened David planned to order in Joab's infantry. Reinforcements and ladders would go up all around the walls of Jerusalem. David mentioned in the war briefing he had hoped this tactic would split King Herod's defense making him try to defend the outer walls of the city, while at the same time trying to stop the wave coming in from the front gate. The company of archers that had fired on the wall had now moved to the tower above the Gate of Gennal and began their arrow assault onto the enemy soldiers below. The King's Palace now belonged to David's forces and was secure. A young Captain of a Thousand named Abishai the brother of Joab and member of the "Thirty" pushed the gates open.

Upon Jerusalem's gates being opened horns blew and the Star of David sat atop the captured tower. When it opened, a contingent of soldiers moved forward to repel David's forces. The fighting there grew fierce, soldiers had fallen all around David and the ground turned red by the spilled blood, but he kept fighting onward in order to clear the entrance for his Cavalry. Smoke filled the air cutting the view of the battlefield. The enemy seemed to be starting to panic as most of them ran screaming away from the battles as we breached the gates. David's forces overran many other spots along the perimeter.

They did not know from which direction David's men would be attacking. From within a General of King Herod attempted to advance to the tower above the wall in order to rally Jerusalem and reclose the gates. The enemy started to push back David's advance. David fought his way towards the captain amongst the battling men and separated his head from his torso with one swing. Upon seeing their commander struck down by the King himself and remembering the legend of King David against the mighty Goliath, Jerusalem's defenders could not stop David from his destiny this day and the hosts bent before his sword. The tower now belonged to David's forces. He had cleared the gate entrance with Joab and the "Thirty".

Commander Joab galloped towards the gates now and ordered the cavalry to charge the city, as they blew past David on their black, brown and white battle tested steeds, he reminded his men to only engage enemy combatants. "Civilians must not be harmed, property must not be destroyed, secure the perimeter and douse the fires. The King is to be taken alive under penalty of death to whom ever lays a finger upon him." After the battle ended the captured said the sight of David's horsemen pouring through the gates in hordes horrified them. It created such a fear in them they claimed to have surrendered Jerusalem to David instantaneously.

David's forces destroyed the remaining pockets of resistance and captured the King to end the fighting. By nightfall Jerusalem belonged to the House of David. King David's soldiers celebrated within the walls of Jerusalem that night. I sat alone in a corner of the banquet hall still soaking in the fact I had just witnessed David's greatest triumph and had not awaken in my own time as of yet. During the battle I had stayed clear enough away to observe everything unfold before me and experienced no fear. I looked now upon all of the "Thirty" clad in their ceremonial gold helmets and black capes save for Joab who had a blue cape; Adino, Eleazer, Shammah the son of Agee, Joab, Abishai, Benaiah, Asahel, Elhanan, Shammah, Elika, Helez, Ira, Abiezer, Mebunnai, Zalmon, Maharai, Heleb, Ittai, Hiddai, Benaiah the Pirathonite, Abi-albon, Azmaveth, Eliahba, Shammah the Hararite, Ahiam, Eliphelet, Eliam, Hezrai, Paarai, Igal, Bani, Zelek, Nahari, Ira, Gareb and Uriah ate and drank at the Kings table and chose any residence within the kingdom as their own.

After eating only a small portion of the feast tabled before him and his captains and not a moment before he enjoyed one of Joab's war tales, David retreated to the Kings Chambers for prayer and rest, he called for me to follow. Upon entering the room David dropped to his knees and began to pray, "Dearest Lord, I thank you for the victory you've granted me this day. I pray for the men lost and for you to bless them into your house." David remained in his chambers for the remainder of the night while his men celebrated in the hall. I was glad David had asked me to join him. The men started to get drunk and I felt out of place.

Chapter Three: To the South

For a moment my memories were interrupted as I felt the plane taxi down the runway preparing to take off. I had made it on board or so was meant to believe. Whoever watched my every move might be allowing me to leave in order for me to lead them to my contact in Israel. I knew nothing at this point but I would have to stay cool and be a lab rat for now, but I did not mean to be their sucker for long. I went back to my childhood memories. My memories continued hazily, becoming clearer at moments and then foggier at other times. The following months with David saw the first tasks of his preparation for the future. He told me Jerusalem would be the key to his kingdom now and forever and at all costs should never be taken by or shared with an enemy. The capital city was no longer Hebron, but now Jerusalem. His family and servants moved to the palace at Jerusalem which everyone now called the "City of David". David began to create a strategy guaranteed to ensure the security of this majestic city from attack for decades to come. During this preparation for the future campaign the King of the Sidonian Empire sent messengers and gifts to David after hearing of his victory at Jerusalem. He offered his lands and allegiance to King David. Joab dispatched two of his best infantry divisions to the Sidonian cities of Tyre and Gebal to fortify the cities and prepare for future campaigns and to collect taxes to assist with the conscription of soldiers.

David called on his nephew and supreme General in order to have his plans to increase and protect the young countries borders laid out before him. Joab entered the throne room looking confident, his General's robe of shiny blue silk hung from his shoulders and grazed the marble floors behind him. His blue robe made him stand out from all the other captains now surrounding him with their black robes. They waited to hear what he had in mind for the future. Joab began his report, "My lord our advance scouts returned with news that has assured me our upcoming advances should be successful. We can move our borders as far south as to neighbor Egypt at the plush coastal city of Arish while at the same time containing our old enemies the Philistines along our eastern coast."

"They have reported little to no resistance should be expected during our advance as we push southwards, until we reach the strongholds at Arish and Elath. The Philistines are scattered and cannot muster a force to rival our own. The city of Arish would be an ideal port because of the location in the Sinai on the coast of the waters. The Amelikites are raiding Egyptian towns from across the border and are going unchecked into Egypt due to the instability of the current Pharaoh. Taking Arish should strengthen our relations with the Egyptians and will stop the incursions by the Amelikites and our possessing this city will also keep the Egyptians from campaigning into our lands like they are known to do on the whim of the Pharaoh."

"Conquering Arish would also give us another port for trading with the sand dwellers and the water peoples across the sea. I plan on finishing what Saul did not for our Lord so we can be blessed. I cannot leave an Amalekite alive and will take no bounty. I must destroy them! I will start by moving southward to rid our borders of the Philistine's." As Joab finished his report he sat down at a table across the throne room.

David clapped his hands together at the thought of recovering the Ark from those pesky Philistines. He turned to Joab and said, "Joab, recovering the Ark and bringing it to Jerusalem would be a blessing and would reinforce the Lord's approval, but what of the Egyptian holdings at Gezer? Do we not allow them access to their own city?"

Joab answered back as if he expected the question, "My lord they would be allowed safe passage through our lands, but they will be commanded to stay on the main road which will have a heavy warrior presence. Any incursions would be met with swift retribution. The divisions at Arish would be reinforced by our taking of the Red Sea port city Elath. Elath is located in the Sinai as well on the coast of the Gulf. My lord this city would give us access to the trade markets with the exotic Nubian cities."

David smiled as he congratulated Joab, "You have conceived a beautiful battle plan. Your plans should create wealth and stability in the south as well as here. Campaign southward and I will hold all other campaigns off until your return to Jerusalem. May The Lord bless you on your campaign and grant you speedy success. Absalom will sit with you tomorrow."

Joab was leaving the throne room when David mentioned Absalom. He turned back around quickly as if someone had stuck a dagger in his back. Absalom was not David's oldest son or heir to the throne, but he loved to fight. When he was younger David would watch him plan attacks with his Captains and often attended Absalom's training sessions.

David then said to Joab, "I am giving Absalom command of a cavalry regiment under your watchful eye."

Joab looked anxious as he spoke rather defiantly to David, "My lord taking Absalom along on this dangerous campaign would be a mistake. In his youth I do not trust he will be able to command this type of element nor do I want to be responsible for Absalom's safety."

He approached the king, "My King, Absalom is a great leader and will make you proud on the battlefield. However, I do believe that he will not follow the orders that I might give to him and I cannot promise his safety to you."

David replied, "What are your concerns Joab?"

Joab responded, "Sir he is too aggressive. He looks to extend his name in battle to rival even yours."

David cut Joab short, "Joab, I understand. Command him as supreme commander but you will not be held responsible for his safety. I will speak with him regarding his discipline."

"Thank you my lord" said Joab. He turned and left for his southerly campaign.

Joab left Jerusalem with ten thousand Infantry, two thousand Archers, one thousand Cavalry soldiers under the direct command of Absalom and five hundred Chariots. His march sent him to the fortress at Arish via an eastward campaign against the Philistines and ending in Elath. He took the route that lead him past and into the Israeli cities of Hebron,

BeerSheba, Gerar, Sharuhen and Raphia to resupply before making the battle run towards the protected port at Arish. Back at home David started becoming restless and talked about expanding westward with his own campaign but he discussed the problems and the lack of defenses to protect the kingdom if he dispatched any more offenses with Joab's force moving so far south.

David got interrupted in his throne room one afternoon while he played host to Amnon, his elder son and heir to the throne. A messenger from Joab arrived with incredible news. Joab's move south had been effective at pushing the Philistines east towards the coast. Joab sent word to David informing him the Ark of the Covenant's journey to Jerusalem would now be unhindered and asked for instructions on how to proceed.

David turned to me as if in shock, "Moosie, (he had finally come around to calling me by my nickname) the Ark's presence in Jerusalem shows the Lord is with me and no enemy would dare attack a stronghold with the Ark present. The Lord has seen fit to bless my Kingdom so I shall personally ride to bring it back." He sent a message to Joab to continue with his advance. He travelled to the house of Abinadab to retrieve the Ark with his priests and a grand procession. I shuttered, was I to witness the Ark's voyage to Jerusalem? Would I be permitted to lay eyes on the Holiest of Relics? No matter what, I had to keep dreaming I did not want to wake up now and miss this.

David called for all of his priests and his personal guard along with a brigade of soldiers to travel with him to secure the Ark. I had never seen him this happy before. The day came when we arrived at the house of Abinadab and the Ark.

David looked towards me and said, "Moosie, you will accompany me into the home to see the Ark."

I stuttered, "Me my King. I do not believe I am worthy of such an audience…I am scared."

David laughed, "We all are in its presence; just remember your fear and you won't have a problem, come."

We walked into a small house of timber and clay brick. We followed Abinadab far down the hall towards a room in the rear of the home. With every step my heart pounded like it was going to explode from my chest. I had to take short controlled breaths so I didn't hyperventilate. My thoughts went to my Grandfather, his father and everyone before him that would have loved to share this moment. As we entered the room holding the presence of the Ark, the air turned electric. I took no more than one step into the room and dropped to my knees crying and touched my head to the ground. I tried to meld with the dirt floor of the clay home to show obedience and fear of the Lord. I mustered the courage to glance to my side and saw David sobbing on his knees. We both fell humbled before the Ark and praised the Lord.

Two boxes sat in this room. One made of gorgeous cedar with beautiful hand carvings of Cherubs sitting on the four corners of the top. The box was polished and sat with carrying poles already attached. The other was a large gold chest with golden cherubs and looked exactly as it was portrayed in the "Raiders of the Lost Ark". Inscriptions were written all over both boxes in Hebrew. I could not understand what the writings said, but I knew It was from God almighty himself.

David looked towards me and whispered, "There are two Arks here because each one serves a different purpose. The gold Ark is our battle Ark and defeats any enemy host before us. The cedar Ark carries the Lord's law and stays with the priests. Neither Ark can be touched by man or he be struck down on the spot. The poles are the only part of the Ark's to be handled by man. Only my priests are allowed to carry either Ark to mount on its wagon. We will leave here for Jerusalem in the morning, the Ark's shall be loaded then." We both left the presence of the Ark's and went in the front room with Abinadab.

Abinadab clasped his hands together and began to speak, "Sir's I have arranged sleeping quarters for you here. I would be honored if you stayed the night within my home. I am blessed to have the Lord, the Ark, King David, his unusual young guest and a host of the Kings finest warriors all with me tonight. A man could not ask for anything more in his lifetime, good night dear sirs." He bowed low and left our room. I had seen the Ark of the Covenant, even if this is a dream I would remember this visit forever. A young man from Philadelphia had kneeled before history, unbelievable.

I laughed in amazement to myself as sleep overcame me. What has the Lord in store for me?

The next morning a buzz filled the air and everyone ran to and fro preparing for the Arks movement from the house to the carts. David gave orders to the priest to be careful and they all knew not to touch them out of fear for their lives. Everything moved slowly now. Young commanders Uzzah and Ahio closely guarded the caravan.

I remained in complete awe as we made our way towards Jerusalem. David had his minstrels play music, sing, dance and clap along the route in celebration of the Ark's return to the city. My eyes stayed glued to them. We moved slowly, but they still shook and tilted on the carts. I began to get concerned that one may fall over. I dare not mention this to David. I probably was just being overly cautious, as I usually am. Several times along the way the priests balanced the poles. I stopped worrying because everyone was doing their jobs.

We had reached a very hilly and rocky area. A treacherous mix for our travel with the Arks and the priest's ability to keep them balanced. I turned around to check on them again and witnessed one of History's bravest yet under appreciated moments. The battle Ark tilted incredibly to the side, it was definitely going to fall. The priests scattered for none dared to touch the Ark, I yelled for David. As he turned towards the Ark I noticed captain Uzzah's eyes. David and Uzzah shared a glance that showed the love of this young warrior for his King. He kept his gaze on David as he stuck out his hand and caught the Ark from falling. He sat the Ark up on the cart. No sooner had he finished, he dropped dead on the spot.

I could not believe what I witnessed. I wondered if I would have done the same thing Uzzah had just done. His brother Ahio ran to him and screamed in pain. David dropped to his knees and began to cry for the young man as I wept for him as well. His bravery saved a nation. The Lord's wrath would have been great, but Uzzah burdened himself with God's anger and died for his King. David proclaimed Uzzah a hero and named the entire area after him for his devotion to the Kingdom. Perez Uzzah was visited yearly by the priests to commemorate the day Uzzah saved Israel from damnation. The Arks made it safely to the city of Jerusalem after a few months of slow travel and were set in Tents. David placed a company of guards around them day and night and no one could go near the Tents save for the priests looking after their welfare.

This dream, voyage or whatever kept me from my family for what seemed like decades but I didn't grow any older while everyone around me did. I just remember taking everything in as if I were a sponge soaking up all the knowledge and wisdom from David. I missed everyone dearly, although I needed to know how this journey played out. As the years went by David and I listened to tales of Joab's southerly conquests. We also heard of Absalom's bravery. Absalom became ferocious in battle and killed without remorse. Joab had managed to take El Arish. The Amelikites dug in and defended their homes to the last man. The fort at Arish turned into a prosperous addition for the Israelites.

When Joab moved on Elath, the enemy didn't fight as hard as they did at El Arish. He left large garrisons at both ports and returned to Jerusalem to brief the king of his successes. Joab came home three years after his initial departure and reported as far south as El Arish, Elath and all in between fell under the command of the house of David. He briefed David on everything that happened along his southerly march. He started to talk about his nephew Absalom. Absalom was not loved by Joab, but tolerated because of his Princely tag. The King's son had become a hero and an outstanding tactician. With the south secure, the time had come for the northern and western borders to be expanded. David charged Joab to create a westward advance strategy to rival his southernly successes. David then told Joab of his plans to promote Absalom to General and have him lead a northern attack.

Joab disagreed with this decision, "My lord I do not think Absalom is quite ready for the responsibility of commanding a campaign. He only just recently commanded his first cavalry regiment. He is impatient, his impatience and over aggressiveness are vices that threaten any strategy created by him. He must remain a captain under my tutelage!"

David responded, "I understand your concerns dear nephew, but he must gain experience as a commander by being in command. I will allow him the northern advance."

Later after Joab had left the throne room David turned to me and spoke as so only I could hear him, "Moosie, I trust Joab with the day to day command of the forces, but I might feel safer having another General, my son Absalom whom has a vested interest in the kingdom also protecting it. He would put down any rebellion that may come against me. Promoting Absalom will be the solution to the problem of Joab influencing the entire force to revolt."

I shook my head in agreement as I said, "David, Absalom's promotion seems necessary for the security of your reign as king over Israel. Joab has too much control over the army as you said. He loves you dearly and would not do anything to harm you; although you never know what secret thoughts a man keeps."

Chapter Four: The Undertaking of a Lifetime

When Joab had completed the plans for his western campaign he came to the throne room and unveiled them to King David. Joab didn't speak in his usual low tones, today he was loud as he spoke, "My King, we should stretch the borders to Medeba and move my forces south to Aroer ending the southern advance in Kir Moab."

David answered his nephew perplexed, "Your plan is to push west and then go southwest? Wouldn't it be wiser to start westward from Elath and attack upward?"

Joab replied confidently, "Lord I fear if I start the campaign from the south and travel north the enemy could continue to retreat only to amass a larger force. Fighting a cornered opponent may be disastrous, especially with the amount of men the Moabite and Edomites have. The current strategy attacks them at their strength early and moves south mopping up pockets of resistance. Upon taking Kir Moab I would then push north through Rabbath-bene-ammon and Mahanaim to Ramath Gilead stopping at the Syrian border in order to regroup and consolidate my forces with Absalom's in preparation for the strike on Damascus."

David smiled and said, "Joab, this is why you are the supreme commander. I have total faith you will succeed. You are dismissed." David turned to me and said, "Now we wait for Absalom." Absalom called for David and Joab's audience a few weeks after Joab unveiled his plans to the king. Absalom stood tall and confident as he discussed his plans with David and Joab.

Absalom began to speak "Father, Commander Joab, it is my intention to attack the fort at Megiddo first for I believe it is the crossroads for traders approaching from the East, West, North and South. The cities

21

of Chinnereth, Hazor, Abel-beth-maacah all the way to Tell Dan will be seized and garrisoned before I turn towards Damascus to assist Joab in his assault on the Assyrians. I plan to use the garrisons at Tyre and Gebal to reinforce my campaign and to help with the attack on Tell Dan."

David approached Absalom and placed his hand on Absalom's shoulders and started to speak, "Son your northern campaign is bold."

Joab then spoke, "I hate to interrupt but Megiddo is heavily fortified and should be assaulted by a commander with more experience than Absalom."

Absalom turned and met Joab's icy stair as he answered Joab's remarks, "Commander Joab, I can take Megiddo and continue north."

Joab cut him short, "I am sure you believe this Absalom, but the truth remains we cannot afford a defeat at such an early stage of the northern campaign."

Absalom responded sarcastically, "Well commander Joab it is impossible for you to be in the South campaigning and at Megiddo commanding."

"Enough!" David yelled as he plopped down onto the throne. "Megiddo is a vital crossroads city and has to be secured from the Philistines and garrisoned immediately. I will lead the attack on Megiddo. Absalom you will continue with your forces north to Chinnereth and follow your plans as you have prepared them. Moosie, ride with me to Megiddo."

David then pointed at Joab and said, "I command you both to create flags for each of your divisions so we can identify our units on a battlefield. This will help against any confusion when we are combined. These commander standards shall be flown above the unit identifiers. The commander standard will be flown under the flag of the Kingdom, do you understand me?"

Absalom and Joab both answered simultaneously, I had never seen David this angry shoot I replied too, "Yes my King." They turned and left as David shooed them away with his hand.

Joab created his standard as a gold Star of David on a black background to honor the men of the thirty. Absalom chose the Star of David in blue with a white background. I thought this was odd and an obvious stab at Joab because his commanding robe was blue and here was Absalom toting a blue Star of David commander standard. The standards were prepared by the seamstresses of Jerusalem and distributed to the ranks before their departure for the foreign battlefields. It took months to gather the supplies and hire the men needed for the three forces, but finally the day of departure was at hand.

On the eve of their departures at the conclusion of the final preparations for the assaults, David and his young Generals knelt to pray before leaving to prepare their forces. They knew these campaigns were the most ambitious they had ever planned. They were going to try and triple their countries size with one coordinated effort. David prayed,"Lord, please bless your hosts with victory. We fight to carry out your will and ask for assistance and mercy. As we walk towards the valley of death we shall fear no evil."

As they rose to leave the throne room they all looked upon each other as if it would be the last time. David handed Absalom his blue Commander's Robe and spoke softly, "My son, I am proud as a father to hand you this and say it is well deserved. It also saddens me to place this weight upon you. If you do not survive this, I will never forgive myself."

Absalom smiled and said, "Father, do you forget I am Absalom, I will not perish in combat for the Lord is with me." He left the throne room with his captains in tow.

As he was leaving a servant walked into the room holding a plate of peanuts and her voice grew loud above everyone, "Peanuts beverages, sir would you like some peanuts or a beverage?"

I opened my eyes and stared out of the plane window overlooking water. I recalled the dreams more vividly and they caused me to be unaware of surroundings when I came back to my senses. We were still flying somewhere over the Atlantic Ocean. The young stewardess stood by my seat holding the tray low and offered me something. I replied to her question, "No, I am ok. Sorry I was daydreaming."

Just then she grabbed a pack of peanuts and shoved them into my hands as she said, "Sir here are the nuts you asked for earlier." I pushed the peanuts back into her hand when I realized there was a note tightly wrapped around them.

I accepted the peanuts and replied, "Thank you I forgot I had asked for these. The stewardess smiled and continued her trek down the aisle offering refreshments to the other passengers.

I opened the folded piece of paper slowly and read the address written on it. ***155 Hayarkon Street Room 212.*** I turned around to see if anyone had seen me take the note. I felt as if a weight had been lifted from my chest. Finally I was to meet with the person or persons who had been helping me all these years, or at least I had hoped. I tried not to think of what the future had in store for me but instead went back to the dreams of the greatest undertaking of David's lifetime. I recalled the moment we left for our campaign.

Joab moved out of the city first to a parade. His army spread four miles silently behind him flying the new standards of the gold star over the black backdrop. As ordered, David's gold star over the sky blue background flew above Joab's standard. They left the city and headed for the Dead Sea via Bethany. The black Commander's Standards were frightful and I imagined the terror of the enemy who had to look upon it before their doom.

Absalom departed the next day, they trumpeted loudly under their standards of a blue star on a white backdrop. His army stretched four miles behind him chanting his name. He headed for the Jordan River passing through Jericho. He would lead them north following the river to Chinnereth so they would have the water needed to travel fast and hard. Absalom's Commander's Standards reminded me of the Israeli flag of my own time. Was it a coincidence his Standards are used instead of David's? I did not mention this fact to David or anyone else.

David and I were the last to leave. Three days after Joab's departure David made his way out of the city. His grand army stretched seven miles behind him under the gold star on the sky blue backdrop; they headed for the city of Megiddo via Shechem. His fifty thousand soldiers left the city to the grandest parade. Trumpets blew from the beginning of the procession until the last soldier left the city gates. David would travel through Bethel and stop at Shechem on the way to Megiddo. David was aware the battle for Megiddo could be twice as hard as the battle for Jerusalem. Once past the mountain ranges the flat lands provided no natural cover for his men and a river surrounded the city of Megiddo so a siege would be out of the question.

David spoke as he looked into the distance with a squint in his eye as if bothered by smoke or some unforeseen problem. "Moosie Megiddo is going to be a tough battle. Stay with my Chariot and do not follow me into combat less we both shall perish."

I replied emotionally because I had spent so much time with David and I shared an indescribable bond with him. "My lord I have been with you since Jerusalem, I will fight by your side. To live or to die, I will be beside you in this battle." David smiled, but I knew he felt no comfort.

He smiled as he replied, "You are not the scared child far away from home hiding at the bottom of my chariot." He clapped his hands and two servants came forth one of which carried a small highly polished wooden box. David turned to me and said, "Moosie this is yours, you have earned it." I remembered opening the present and becoming a man as I pulled out my own Black Silk Robe. David placed his hand on my shoulder as the servants helped me put on and clasp the robe. He then said, "Mustafa, welcome to the Thirty!"

I dropped to one knee and replied, "David, I will cherish this forever." I wanted desperately for this not to be a dream. I wanted to take my robe with me back home so everyone knew my journey to manhood had been completed. When I awoke my robe would be gone and everything around me would disappear. I smiled because the memory of this moment could never be taken from me. The entire day I rode behind David on the other gift given to me. A Black Arabian Steed whom I named Falazel. I thought of what responsibilities my new robe and status with the Thirty now meant for me.

Chapter Five: Megiddo

The Philistines were hardy opponents and knew of our approach. Scouts had reported Philistine reinforcements gathering in The Plains of Sharon near Dor. We had to stay at Shechem for a few weeks to organize the attack on Megiddo. This would be one of David's greatest assaults, one for the ages. Upon reaching Shechem David sent for his Captains to plan the assault. I did not stay at the usual place off to the side where I usually heard his speeches. My black robe now reserved me a seat with the Captains at the table.

When everyone sat down David began to speak, "Men, as you are aware Megiddo is approachable by three routes; the Egyptian Pharaoh Thutmose III conquered Megiddo and in doing so named each route. The first path is named Yokneam. This would take us westward through Dor pass a small village called you guessed it, Yokneam. We then have to travel to Bethlehem where we would still have to move down to the plains of Megiddo. The next route is named the Aruna route. This is a narrow path cutting through the mountains and into a valley making us vulnerable to archer attacks from the mountain ridges above. This route would also take away the advantage of our massive numbers because we would have to travel double file into the Valley. The third route is named Taanakh. This path will go through Dothan and around the mountains approaching Megiddo from the east with our army facing the Sea. The Taanakh route is the most fortified by our enemy but is the quickest way to the Megiddo plains. Our route of attack can be decided by our enemies' defenses on each path. We will wait here in Shechem for the report and decide which way to travel after deliberating on the news."

After the meeting he sent men to watch the three approaches. Weeks later the scouts returned with their reports. They were as follows; two divisions of infantry, each with three thousand men sat outside of Dor in the Plains of Sharon. They defended any attempt to take the Yokneam Route to Bethlehem. They were in reserve to the one thousand archers hidden along the top of the Aruna Route's mountain valley pass. The two thousand Chariots and two divisions of infantry with three thousand men in each settled at the end of the pass defending Megiddo. The Taanakh Route was protected by two divisions of infantry with three thousand men per division outside of Dothan along with one thousand Archers, two thousand Chariots and a division of three thousand infantry in reserve.

In all twenty seven thousand soldiers defended Megiddo. David outnumbered them two to one. His strength did not comfort him because of the terrain and the tenacity in which the Philistines often fought with. Their ferocity alone made his superiority in numbers a must. His attack plan had to use his numbers to their full advantage and exploit the enemy's tactics of separating their army to defend three approaches. In the meantime David made it so the Philistine scouts reported his forces were at Shechem and would use the Eastern Road as our approach to Megiddo.

David's route selection prompted the Philistine commander to move his units from the Plains of Sharon to the Megiddo plains. He kept his units in their current division sizes to be more mobile, larger units like David's did not respond as fast as the smaller ones to battlefield demands.

On the morning of the battle the weather was perfect. The sun shone brightly in the sky as the breeze cooled the sparsely vegetated plains as it swept off the ocean onto the gathered opposing forces outside of Dothan. We sat for awhile gazing at the enemy when David realized the men assembled could not be the fighting force. He laughed and said, "Old dog, he thinks I am fooled by his show of force. These men before us won't fight. They will run and join the main body as soon as we move against them. He will give me Dothan in order to combine his army to save Megiddo." David ordered his archers to approach and engage the enemy. Two divisions of infantry accompanied them. As soon as they moved out to engage the Philistines, we noticed their retreat.

They did exactly what David had said they would do. He clapped his hands in approval and said, "Ha, I knew it. I would have done the same thing. The Philistines wish to combine their forces on the plains of Megiddo.

I will see them there after we take Dothan." David ordered all units to move into Dothan. The city put up no resistance. He then waited for scouts to report back what the plains of Megiddo currently held for him. They reported the Philistine troops were on the plains in defensive array awaiting our arrival.

We moved to the Megiddo Plains. A smaller army divided into more divisions stood before us. Their smaller division sizes meant they moved faster than we did, but David's war plans consisted of beating them with brute force and massive numbers. The opposing forces stood on the battlefield facing each other in the quietness. David would be the first to order movement. He ordered his archers to fire on the opposing archers while the infantry advanced to attack the enemy archer units.

Like a well-commanded unit the Philistine archers marched backwards out of range of David's archers and fired upon the advancing infantry division. The Philistine Infantry divisions marched towards David's infantry divisions double-teaming the flanking troops while bogging down the center division holding it up to make it vulnerable to archers. David knew as I did this tactic would cause his demise. The Philistine's attempted to control the flanks and surround David's men. They sent all their units to attack the flanks leaving the center as an avenue for the chariots to attack David's archers. David's face showed his dislike of the current positioning of his units and he ordered his cavalry into the fray.

The cavalry protected the archers who fired upon the approaching chariot division. They met the enemy chariots in the middle of the battlefield amongst a barrage of arrows. David's archers redirected their fire to the center infantry battle where David's infantry held the upper hand. The Philistine chariots did not match up well with David's cavalry. The remaining chariots retreated to the Philistine commander for new instructions. David's combined cavalry losses numbered just below three thousand. He ordered them to attack the center of the Philistine advance. His Chariots converged with the Cavalry and together with the infantry they broke through the middle annihilating the defending Philistine division.

David's flanking infantry Divisions were not fairing so well. All attention had gone to aiding the middle skirmish. The flank divisions held but lost a lot of ground. The Philistine commander pulled his archers and retargeted the flanks. The enemies reserve units joined the battle on their respective flanks and aided in pushing back David's advance. David's divisions faced three Philistine divisions each. The five thousand man divisions of David defended against three, three thousand man Philistine divisions, all the while being fired upon by archers

David ordered his flanking infantry to retreat, as they did they pulled the Philistine divisions toward them and into a bad position and they became outflanked by the center units now mopping up and moving towards the Archers. David's archers were being decimated. He ordered the chariots to split into companies and engage the enemy archer units. The Philistine commander ordered the rest of his chariots and personal guard to defend the archer divisions. The ensuing chariot battle was one of the hardest fought on those plains. Many men and horses were trampled under chariots or bludgeoned. Later that evening David disclosed to me the carnage was unlike any he had ever seen in his career. The chariots managed to destroy one entire archer division, but at a hefty toll. David lost five thousand chariots, the remaining chariots regrouped in the rear.

Having one of his archer divisions completely destroyed he ordered his last archer division inside the city walls. David ordered his center infantry division to reinforce the left division by attacking the right flank of the enemy, while ordering all other forces except a cavalry division to converge with the right Philistine units. This move divided the Philistine's army into two pockets. The right side, under attack and being decimated by David's combined forces, and the left side, now evenly matched and slowly being forced backwards. The Philistine commander now completely vulnerable to a cavalry attack blew his horn and ordered a full retreat into the city. Only two divisions made it inside the Megiddo walls, the rest were lost. David ordered his units to hold off any more attacks until the next day. It started getting dark and the men rested and ate what they could despite all the carnage before them.

Not long after the battle David ordered for the dead to be removed from the battlefield and buried. I had not seen the bodies in Jerusalem because I had been whisked away to the safety of the throne room as I hid in the chariot. My heart saddened as I saw the bloodied corpses and dismembered limbs. So many lives lost never to live again; I now understood the weight of a King. The burdensome responsibility of so many lives tied to your daily decisions. After the cleanup David planned the siege of Megiddo. He ordered scouts to the surrounding roads to ensure no enemy divisions in reserve lurked about. He gave the men an entire day to rest and prepare for the next day.

We took inventory of the remaining force. The losses the Philistine commander caused him seemed to trouble David. Of the fifty thousand total soldiers he left Jerusalem with he only had thirty four thousand left. David had lost sixteen thousand men in one day. The Philistine's started the war with twenty seven thousand soldiers. They were decimated down to six thousand five hundred soldiers. They lost twenty thousand five hundred soldiers in the battle on the plains. In all there were thirty six thousand five hundred dead littered over the battlefield.

We stood staring at each other without saying if Absalom had been the Commander on this day; the northern campaign would have stalled here at Megiddo. He could not have won this battle. My thoughts went to his son and Joab who conducted their own campaigns. David began to say a prayer for their success and safety as if reading my mind. For the first time since before the fighting he spoke to me in a low and tired voice, "This campaign was one of the hardest I have ever commanded. This Philistine has a great understanding of tactics and warfare." I nodded still a little dazed from the battle with a horrified blank face as I gazed once more at the dead and wounded on the battlefield.

A moat surrounded the walls of Megiddo. The city had an outer and inner wall for even more fortification. A protected water supply meant they could withstand a siege for longer than David wanted to be assembled on the plains in front of the city. He needed a plan to get them out and to make it his. The Philistine commander readied the remaining soldiers for the imminent attack. The Tabira Gate and the West Gate seemed the most vulnerable and led directly to the city. He mustered his last archers atop the Inner Walls and spread his remaining infantry amongst the two gates.

David looked upon the Megiddo walls and reminisced with me of our assault on Jerusalem. He told his captains this city had more formidable defenses and a much abler commander than did Jerusalem when we attacked. David continued to speak on how Megiddo was the "doorway to Jerusalem". He told them Megiddo had to be conquered to fortify Jerusalem and to control the trade routes throughout the area. He ordered his archers to dip their arrows in oil and burn them before firing upon the walls and into the city. He discussed with his commanders of his plans to conduct a long arrow assault on the walls to create fear in the soldiers and to keep them huddled behind their walls. He would also move his infantry into assault position under the guise of darkness. Everyone agreed the night and the constant arrow bombardment would be sufficient cover to protect the infantry's movements.

David ordered shields to cover the battering rams and their crews protecting them from arrows and burning oil. He then moved archers near the Tabira and West gates to assault the guards while his forces moved to attack the doors. Shields covered the entire infantry divisions around the gates while the archers continued their barrage of the walls. David ordered his chariot and cavalry to join the assault, so they rode back and forth firing arrows at the wall as well. The city defenders didn't want to stand up for fear of an arrow piercing their bodies. Everyone with the nerve to do so died on the spot with arrows in his torso. David succeeded in moving his entire force to the gates without losing a man and scared the enemy from the walls.

As the sun rose David allowed his trademark trumpets to blow loudly. The trumpets sent them into more of a panic. The order to assault the gate doors sounded and a loud and thunderous boom from the rams hitting the gates with tremendous force vibrated throughout the city. David's forces began singing in time to the booms, I found myself singing with them, "*Sing Praises to The Lord, Sing Praises Sing Praises. Sing Praises to our King, Sing Praises Sing Praises.*" The Philistines left their defenses of the wall in droves now petrified of the blood crazed Israelites at their gates singing. Upon the gates being destroyed we ran into Megiddo unchallenged. The entire Philistine army surrendered and gave their allegiance to King David whose men sang his praises. Megiddo now fell under his command. He ordered his captains to secure the Fortress and thanked The Lord for letting him be victorious yet again. Everyone wanted to go home, but what worried me the most was when I thought of home I thought of Jerusalem, not Philly?

Chapter Six: Bathsheba

With Megiddo taken and now garrisoned with thousands of Israelites the region stabilized. David and I traveled happily to Jerusalem. We did not worry about anything because Absalom was making his way north and all enemy troops moved to stop his northward thrust or had been routed in defeat. David arrived back into Jerusalem to a grand parade. David dispatched scouts for reports of both his General's progress as soon as we returned.

What seemed like two months had passed when the first scout came back with news from the west. Joab had secured and fortified Medeba, Aroer and all cities south. He now stood poised to assault Rabbath-bene-Ammon and asked if David wanted to be present for the victory at the city. He also wanted word of David's campaign against Megiddo. David sent back news that all went well and Megiddo will prove to be important to the kingdom of Israel's existence in the future.

David turned to me, "Mark my words Moosie, Megiddo will prove to be vital to Jerusalem's survival. Megiddo must always be garrisoned."

I placed a hand upon David's shoulder and said to him, "I have travelled this road with you. I too am aware of the importance Megiddo holds." David told Joab he would leave Jerusalem with his guard and should be with him within a full moons span, a month more or less I figured.

Before David and I departed for the battle front with Joab we sat many a night and talked of my time and how it differed from his. He was astonished at the ways the human race had developed over the years and showed his distaste for the fast living. He called it a lust to be Gods and frowned at the lack of humanity we displayed for each other. I thought it funny coming from the foreskin reaper. While sitting on the roof of the palace I noticed a young woman sunbathing and taking hot baths in sight of the palace.

I noticed David had especially enjoyed the moments when she interrupted our conversations with her evening ritual. I had not known he had asked for her to be brought to the palace to be introduced to him. This began a series of events I expected, but still had no idea of how a woman blinded even the wisest and righteous of men. Right before our trip to visit Joab, David found love with a woman of exceptional intelligence and beauty named Bathsheba the wife of a member of the "Thirty". Their times together were some of the only moments David sent me away from his side. During this time a scout returned with news Absalom had advanced north and now moved southwestward to link with Joab's divisions to provide a united defense against the Assyrians who aggressively stood against Israel. David received word from Joab when it came time for his visit with the troops at Rabbath-bene-Ammon to give them the motivation to continue their assault into Damascus.

David's trip to the front seemed to inspire and ignite him with a sense of pride. Our travels went through lands David had never been. One thing was evident, the people loved him wherever we visited. Parades followed us throughout our journey. King David had created an empire in his lifetime to be rivaled only by the Egyptians. The Lord had delivered in his promise to David. In his speech to Joab's soldiers he promised when they returned home they would be heroes for all time. He promised their sons would never have to fight the epic battles they are being asked to because of the hard work and victories they were now providing.

On the return to Jerusalem as we both rode ahead of the detachment David confided with me that Bathsheba haunted his thoughts. He hoped he proved strong enough to resist the temptations so many of us submitted to. At the time my youth did not permit me to understand his struggle to fight his insane desire for Bathsheba. I had a funny feeling I would get a crash course in women soon enough though.

David stared into the distance as he talked to me, "Moosie you are yet a child so the affairs of men and women are foreign to you. I will tell you this though. Adam had his Eve and lost his favor with the Lord for her. I hope to not lose mine for Bathsheba. Pray for me."

I responded softly for I understood by the look on his face that a great burden laid with him, "My King and friend, the Lord will remain with you forever and favor has never been lost, thus my visit here confirms." David smiled as he turned his horse to ride back to the caravan moving slowly towards Jerusalem. "Still be righteous!" I yelled after him, he showed no sign he had heard me over the gallop of his horse. I then whispered, "Still be righteous my King."

Shortly after our return to Jerusalem rumors of David and Bathsheba's affair began to move around the kingdom. I had suspicions but when she got pregnant it became apparent. Those of us in the King's inner circle knew he had become desperate to marry her before she gave birth. He talked of it often in private. He talked mostly about how he could not wed a woman already married, so he had to find a way to make her unmarried as he would put it. Several ideas came to mind in our discussion to make her available, but one seemed more plausible than the others. David and I expected vicious battles still to come for Joab's forces in the west. David commented he would order Joab to assign him to a unit on the front lines and arrange for his death. The events leading up to Bathsheba's husband's demise showed me to the ruthless side of David. My part in this plan did not provide me any comfort either. I probably should have stopped the madness but I did nothing. It took some time to forgive myself. I forgave David for his betrayal later in life because I realized he was only a human man and we all do stupid things in the name of love.

The weeks and months following his instructions to Joab regarding Uriah I visited with David as he worried like never before about the battle for Damascus and the Assyrians.

"Moosie, if Joab and Absalom fail to put down the Assyrians they will march straight for Jerusalem. We need to place early warning units on the roads." David said to me as he fixed his gaze on a torch in the corner of the throne room.

"My King, don't worry about the Assyrians. They have Joab and Absalom to deal with. I doubt anything but total victory will be reported." I assured him. I then hoped the Assyrians didn't realize they would win by just standing aside and letting Absalom and Joab Kill each other.

David walked towards a table and grabbed a cup of tea, in between gulps he said, "In any other time you would be right Moosie, but I am ashamed and worried about my favor with the Lord over this Bathsheba matter." He said concernedly now holding his head in his palms.

I walked over and sat at the table, "David, the Lord understands your heart and I am certain punishment will come for any wrong doing. Pray for forgiveness and remain righteous." I stood from the table and left the chamber to allow him to be alone with his thoughts.

Joab's forces soon linked with Absalom's and they took Damascus. Absalom would have driven his troops to the western waters if Joab had not sent word back to David that Absalom continued the push against his orders. David ordered the young Prince back home immediately. Absalom had grown in power and had spies planted in David's royal court. They informed him Joab had a hand in his being dispatched home. Everyone under their commands saw and discussed the hatred they had for each other and their captains mentioned how it was a matter of time before the two clashed. It appeared to me Absalom resented Joab for his position and wanted to prove he could out perform him at every turn. It became common knowledge how Joab did not trust Absalom and everyone also expected when given the opportunity Absalom would turn on Joab.

Joab stayed behind to command the troop placements and garrison construction in defense of the cities they had captured. He assigned competent Captains to each city as mayors. These Captains gathered taxes and guaranteed the general safety of all the occupants. It was during this time Bathsheba was moved into the palace. After all the newly captured and occupied cities were garrisoned Joab returned back to Jerusalem to hold audience with his King and report the new boundaries of Israel.

Joab's visit with David extended deep into the night. Israel had grown quite a bit since they last met. The two caught up on old times, new conquests and a whole new arsenal of war stories from Joab. Joab reported King David's kingdom now spanned cities and treasures untold. The kingdom ran from as far south as El Arish and Eilat to as far west as Damascus and as far north as Tell Dan. Joab described the cities, creatures and people he saw and met along the way. He told the king everything. The old friends agreed peaceful days should be ahead of them for some time. Joab received permission from the king to relax and received two months of leave to spend with his family. David's happiness for Israel's peaceful days only increased as he ordered the supplies of the Temple to be gathered and stored.

Israel's new expansion made incredible tax revenue for the construction of the Temple. David sadly informed me the Lord intended to punish him for his sin against Uriah. Bathsheba's pregnancy had turned difficult and the Lord told him his child with her would die. Another punishment for his transgressions was that he could not be the one to build the Temple. After he informed me of his punishments by the Lord David spent what seemed like months in seclusion to mourn his child's death and to pray for the Lord's forgiveness. Discovering he would not build his lifelong dream and monument to the Lord seemed to tear him apart and I wondered if he would ever truly be the same again.

Chapter Seven: Absalom's Descent

Just then the Airline Pilot's voice came over the speakers asking everyone to take their seats and fasten their seatbelts. We had flown over the Atlantic Ocean and now approached Paris where we had to land and pick up travelers connecting to Israel and dropping off those going to Paris. I could only imagine modern day Jerusalem. Granted I had never been to Israel, but with such vivid dreams I wanted to compare them with the real thing. As the plane landed in Paris I peered out to find the Eiffel Tower. The Airport Tarmac filled the window so I closed my eyes and went back to my memories. I resumed at a happier point when David called for his son Absalom to return home from his campaigns and asked Absalom to brief him. Absalom visited his father and discussed in detail every aspect of the northern campaign.

Absalom entered the throne room in a flurry and started to speak, "The many lands I conquered are as diverse and rich as any I have ever seen you defeat. We spilled much blood and in some cases had to kill entire armies leaving none alive!"

David asked, "My son why would you kill an entire army? All they fight for is the right to rule their own lands."

Absalom replied, "I had to send a message to the next army. I will not accept defeat and I will destroy their lands. Anyone who stands against me must perish."

David stood and approached Absalom, "Son I am happy you are victorious and such a feared leader and General, but it disappoints me you get so much joy in killing. Your hands are as bloody as mine."

He gazed over at me deeply troubled because if anything ever happened to Amnon, Absalom would expect to compete for the throne with his older brothers. Everyone expected Amnon to rule upon David's death. We had no idea at the time some of Absalom's Captains started swearing allegiance to their young prince against David. David levied harsh taxes on the land in order to provide the necessary monies to purchase the supplies for the Temple. The tribal chiefs complained how many citizens felt a financial strain under David's new taxation policies and added the people were not happy with him, thus allowing for Absalom's treachery.

David and I heard rumors regarding Amnon and his apparent rape of Tamar, David's daughter with one of his other wives and Absalom's youngest and dearest sister. David punished Amnon for the crime but Absalom carried much hatred for his brother and upon verifying the accuracy of the story ordered Amnon to be killed. All of Absalom's brothers feared him and worried his rage would go unchecked by their father. Absalom's brothers fled Jerusalem because they believed he wanted them killed as well.

When Joab informed David of Amnon's murder, David fell to the ground heartbroken. He ordered Joab to bring Absalom before him, but he had already fled the country and found safe haven in Geshur, the kingdom of his mother. Amnon the eldest son lay dead and no clear heir to David's throne existed. David took some time to mourn Amnon before he began to search once again for an heir. David's next capable son Adonijah was smart and only fourteen, but David had said Adonijah's quietness hurt him and he felt that his son was easily manipulated by others. Adonijah would have to impress upon his father his independence and strong will to catch the Kings eye to be heir. David's younger son Solomon the second child of David and Bathsheba warmed his heart tremendously with his hunger for knowledge and his knack for problem solving.

Solomon was only ten years old at the time, but seemed to always be around watching and learning instead of playing with the other children. He would not shy away from asking me a question or two.

One afternoon while sitting in the throne room playing Chaturanga David leaned over and said to me "Moosie, the other night in chambers with Bathsheba I promised her that Solomon would inherit the throne. Please provide him with the best training from this point forward."

I nodded and said, "Sure David he will be ready when the time comes."

Solomon impressed everyone around him. He learned quickly and once he figured out how to do something he never forgot. We would walk the grounds of the Palace and talk. I did not seem to age in this dream yet as months and years passed everyone else did. A short time after Solomon turned thirteen he stopped me in the Palace.

Solomon pulled me aside and whispered, "Moosie, last night I visited with another time and place as you visit us here."

"Where did you go?" I replied back in the same hushed tone. He seemed thrilled to tell someone.

"I walked the future and the past." He said.

"Did you visit my time?" I asked, almost as anxious for the answer as he was to tell me.

Solomon placed his hand on my shoulder and said, "Moosie I did indeed sit with you, but I cannot tell you anything now. There is still much here for both of us to learn. The time will come when we shall discuss what is to be done." I understood and brought it up no more. We continued to become the best of friends.

Later we found out Absalom planned to rebel. His old regiments proved to be loyal to him and were prepared to act against David if Absalom so ordered. Joab remained vigilante and untrusting of Absalom. He discovered the plot and briefed David and I.

Joab began his tirade as soon as we shut the throne room doors. "My lord, there is word of Absalom mounting a campaign to take Jerusalem by force. His army is massive and he cannot be allowed to muster them. If this rumor is true we must stop him from reaching the city. Let me march out to meet him in battle. Please David, let us deny Absalom the opportunity to march!" Joab shouted.

David held up his hand to quiet Joab and spoke, "Joab, my son shall not gather his forces, go to Geshur, take with you a small detachment as to not bring attention to yourself while you travel. Arrest Absalom and take him to his residence in Jerusalem as a criminal. Keep him from my presence." David started walking out of the room.

As David turned to leave Joab answered in a low voice, "Yes my lord it shall be done." A few weeks later Joab returned to brief David about his mission. It was a success and Absalom had been captured and placed on house arrest and not allowed any communication with the King.

Many years went by without Absalom being able to speak with his father. In the meantime his secret rebellion had grown stronger. He moved back in his fathers good graces but David sent him away from Jerusalem and appointed Absalom judge of the Hebron District. Rumors began to spread how he was now ready to make his move on the kingdom. Later Joab reported Absalom dispatched messages to his supporters letting them know the day and time in which the revolt would be initiated all the while pretending to be obedient to David.

One afternoon David and I sat in the throne room having one of our lively conversations over lunch when the doors burst open and slammed into the walls. We both stood and drew our swords only to see Joab running at us talking in a loud hurried tone, "My lord the time for your departure is at hand; even I cannot protect you from Absalom's forces now. He is much stronger and richer than I and has many more regiments loyal to him. They are on the move and will be here by nightfall." David flopped back down in his chair by the window and stared at the throne as if Joab's words had pierced his soul.

Joab walked hurriedly over to David and placed his hand on David's shoulder and said compassionately, "We must move now with all that are loyal to you and vacate Jerusalem!"

David could barely speak, his voice was choked by tears, "Joab, it has come to this? Have I not been a good King and father to Absalom? I will not run he must kill me to take Jerusalem!"

Joab now angered by David's plummet into what seemed to be a stupor grabbed him and stared directly into his eyes, "David he will not hesitate to kill you, and if that happens; then I most certainly have already been put down. A much better moment for your fight shall come my king, I promise this. We cannot win here! We must leave!"

David wiped the tears from his face and whispered, "Send word to my troops and Generals who are loyal. Tell them to prepare for the escape from the city." He turned to me still wiping his eyes and said, "Moosie what do you think?"

I sat at the table and answered, "David, I believe that if anyone could, you can definitely hold this city."

David sighed, closed his eyes and replied, "So, I am not the only one who believes this."

Joab cut us short though with his reply, "Both of you are very brave, but neither of you know for sure the numbers standing against you. Would it be us three versus the realm? Leaving now to regroup is better than not being able to leave at all later."

That was enough to convince us that it was time to go. We sadly left Jerusalem. I looked behind me and remembered the day when I was delivered to this land and those walls were my first sights with David. I wondered if I would ever lay eyes on Jerusalem again. As if reading my mind David said with sorrow in his voice, "If it is The Lord's will we shall return victorious." I bowed to him and turned Falazel to the unknown trail ahead.

Chapter Eight: A New King

Upon leaving Jerusalem David quickly dispatched his spies. They reported Absalom held Jerusalem with force and the iron fist of fear. Joab sent word to the loyal regiments under David to rally near the city of Mahanaim, outside of the Woods of Ephraim. Months passed before David's forces mustered at Mahanaim, but soon David had a force assembled that could face his son with the ever slight possibility of success. As David and Joab devised their plans to retake Jerusalem, I spent much time in the camp with young Solomon answering his hundreds of questions regarding the situation.

David's spies had managed to work their way into Absalom's advising circle and informed us when Absalom called his Generals to the throne room to discuss his battle plans. It was reported that Absalom said, "Send divisions to find him, let any soldier holding the head of David before me be my General of the guard."

Absalom's advisors warned against this move, one brave advisor and spy for David stepped forward and spoke, "Lord Absalom, we should not waste precious resources looking for David. He will come to us when the time is at hand. We must train and prepare for the imminent attacks."

All reports from the spies showed he had grown bothered by the ignorance and cowardice of his counselors. Absalom walked over to the lone advisor whom had spoken out, with his mouth almost touching the shorter advisors eyes and a vein popping in his temple they reported he screamed, "I cannot wait for his attack on Jerusalem, my father knows this city. He conquered it before; he will not be given another chance."

"Yes my lord as you ordered." said the advisor as he backed away and quietly left the throne room. Two apprentice advisors began arguing over the right choice to make.

The younger of the two spoke, "I don't think we should separate the troops on a wild chase for King David. If they find him I am sure he has enough men to defend himself and we lose those divisions as well as build to the legend of David."

The elder advisor replied, "You have much to learn. Absalom chooses to cut the head from the snake before it strikes."

The younger advisor snickered back, "So you think it wise to search for the snake in its hole and risk the chance of getting bitten by accident or to surprise the snake and set a trap guaranteeing you don't get poisoned?"

"These are military affairs. Your experience is limited in matters of tactics and warfare. Absalom is aware of the dangers and is prepared to meet them!" ended the elder advisor as he turned and walked from the throne room. The spy ended the report to Joab saying Absalom would come for David with all of Jerusalem emptied behind him.

A year and six months passed before David and Joab completed their plans, a plan turning Absalom's aggression against himself. The perfect spot and strategy was devised to use the woods and mountains around the Woods of Ephraim to trap Absalom and take him prisoner. Joab would lead the attack. The plans were laid and now it was time to set the bait. I followed Joab into battle, so I could be there to guarantee Absalom's safety.

As Joab led the troops into position for the attack, he sent word into Jerusalem that King David had been seen in Mahanaim near the Woods of Ephraim drilling. We wanted Absalom to empty Jerusalem once he discovered our location. Our spies confirmed he did just that and informed us how Absalom intended to reach David's force before we set out to march on Jerusalem. Spies also informed Joab about Absalom's counselors warning him this may be a trap and counseling him to stay and prepare Jerusalem to defend against an assault. We knew Absalom's pride and arrogance would make him shun his counselor's advice. I think he actually believed himself smarter in war than David.

It was common knowledge that his father had no match at laying sieges to fortresses but remained vulnerable sometimes at open field battle. I didn't know whether Absalom had word his opponent would be none other than Joab. The last thing the spies reported was that in secrecy Absalom's closest advisors started sending their families from Jerusalem fearing Absalom would not win this battle. Absalom made a beeline across the River Jordan straight towards the Woods of Ephraim. Scouts had returned with warning of Absalom's army being at least a two days ride from the woods. Joab sent his commanders to ready the traps and gave them their pre-battle orders.

He commanded that none were to touch Absalom or face death themselves. With the plans readied and men in position Joab prayed to the Lord for victory to restore his King's house and for him to be reunited with his family in Jerusalem. David waited in Ammon with his small contingent of guards for any news of the encounter. Joab sent a scout to David to inform of Absalom's location and how his troops outnumbered Joab's three to one. Joab gazed over at me and smiled, "This is going to be the fight to secure Israel's borders for decades to come. No matter what the outcome no one would dare field an army against whoever wins."

If Joab won it would make him the most revered and feared General in all the land. He then turned and yelled with a grin "Everyone had better kill your three! Sound the horns we've a war to tend to" Under a cloudy sky, Joab went about the camp lifting the spirits of the troops for the next day's battle. It started to rain heavily.

Joab smiled at me and said, "The Lord has blessed our plans to use these woods as a defensive shield and an offensive weapon. The only effective weapon against the wood is fire and this rain makes fire a non-factor."

Later our spies informed us the rain seemed to cause Absalom great distress. Joab had spies everywhere. We even got a spy report from his battle tent. Absalom in his fury reportedly said, "I want a full scale assault with no reserves held. Show these dogs no mercy because none will be shown to you. Every man standing against me on this field of battle must die! I want their heads in piles for all to witness! Bring David to me!" He walked out of the tent and left his captains to finish the assault plans for the next day's battle without him.

Chapter Nine: The Woods of Ephraim

The next day it turned gray, cold and the rain came down hard and steady. Joab set his archers high into the trees so they had a clear shot path over the entire field. I joined the archers under the large green canopies of leaves serving as umbrellas and concealment for us. As hard as the rain fell I doubted we would have been seen one hundred yards out in the open by the enemy. Our reserve units and three quarters of our infantry hid in the woods. All of us had bows in which to fire upon Absalom's army at Joab's command. His plan consisted of each man killing at least three in order for this campaign to be a success. Shooting from hidden raised positions would be ideal to achieve this. Joab wanted Absalom to count small infantry numbers and to think more men hid in the woods. He hoped the question of where and when they would show up to concern Absalom, as well as how many. He believed this would cause Absalom to hold more men back as reserve than he actually should have.

Absalom's horns sounded and I looked out as his army assumed their attack formations. Our forces stood firm as Absalom's units marched towards us with the blue Star of David flying over the white background; their flags blowing in the wind and rain snapped loudly as they moved to meet us on the field. Their flags blazed brightly while catching the attention of friend and foe for miles and in some cases looked to be glowing. Absalom's forces soon came within arrow range of our troops. "Fire" Joab yelled above the drumming of Absalom's army. Thousands of arrows turned the sky black. I placed an arrow and pulled the string back so far that my arm ached. I let go and watched as it joined the others on its way to the enemy. I placed another on my bow in preparation for their advance.

In a moment Absalom's armies disappeared under their shields. The men who moved too slow fell dead on the spot pierced with arrows. Their army quickened their paces to a charge. I picked out targets and fired down upon them from the tree at will. Our arrow barrage was extremely effective and Absalom lost many men. Joab yelled to the infantry, "Hold men, hold steady until the last possible minute. I want the two armies to clash close to the woods so we can drag their asses into the chaos of the woods." I fired many arrows into Absalom's massive army. This would be my first combat experience where I actually took a life. I seemed tuned into each target and hit with surprising accuracy.

As enemy units entered the woods our reserves ambushed and annihilated them. Absalom started to understand our strategy and ordered his men to fall back, but he acted too late. Joab's Cavalry had already begun a pincer movement to outflank Absalom. Even though Absalom had the superior numbers Joab had managed to enclose them on three sides and pushed inward funneling them into the dense woods. The battle raged on ferociously for most of the day. Absalom's forces refused to be defeated easily.

Late in the afternoon we had gotten the upper hand. Commander Joab and I fell back from the fighting to find Absalom's position on the battlefield and make our way there. We caught site of the young King and galloped with the security detail towards him. Absalom gathered his remaining men for a move that would break open the right flank and allow his forces to reestablish a new front. Joab redirected his forces faster than Absalom mustered his weary men and the battle ended around Absalom in those woods.

Joab's Captains ordered the prisoners to be taken away. Joab sent all except for his closest captains from the woods. The captains formed a circle surrounding Joab and Absalom in the privacy and seclusion of the woods.

"You will not always be here to defend my father." Absalom gloated.

"You assume you will be around to threaten him." Joab answered back.

"Did not my father order for my safe delivery to him?" Absalom asked as he stared at me.

"That was the order, but your father isn't here to enforce it." Joab replied. I heard Joab unsheathe his sword and I turned to look at him. He glanced at me to see whether I planned to interfere.

A part of me wanted to stop this because David had sent me to ensure Absalom's murder didn't happen, but I knew for David's safe reign, it had to happen. I turned my back to Absalom. I made up my mind this madness would end here instead of giving Absalom the opportunity to end it for us one dark night while we slept. I knew David would not punish his son and I did not want Absalom in the shadows plotting to kill every old enemy.

"We settle this here Absalom, we settle this forever." Joab said.

The circle of captains turned their backs as I had done and started beating their swords against their shields. I swung back around in time to catch Absalom unsheathe his sword. Joab lunged for Absalom, but Absalom caught Joab's lunge and countered catching Joab on the arm cutting his shoulder. Joab winced at the pain of his wound and parried Absalom's second thrust and cut across Absalom's chest. Joab prepared to hit Absalom but the young prince got beneath his swing and tackled him. As he and Absalom wrestled he picked up a hand full of dirt without Absalom noticing. Absalom straddled his chest and prepared to deliver a fatal thrust when Joab threw the dirt in his eyes.

With Absalom temporarily blinded Joab jumped at the advantage, he maneuvered behind Absalom and slit his throat. Absalom stood shocked for a moment grasping at his throat as the blood squirted bright red and fell to the ground around him. He smiled at me before falling dead. News of the outcome got back to David. Absalom's death in battle saddened him. He questioned not the circumstances of Absalom's fall but only grieved for his son. Joab left a considerable garrison in Amman. This extended David's western borders and gave him a four to five day warning of any advancing enemy.

David ordered the flags of Absalom to be flown at half-mast to pay tribute to his son's death for a little while. The journey back to Jerusalem was a sad one. David and I barely talked as he mourned. He told me he had never got a chance to talk to his son before his death. He wanted the chance to tell Absalom he still loved him. He also mentioned how he felt ashamed of his family and wondered why he should lose sons to each other and in battle. He spoke of the Lord's promise to keep his family safe and did not understand this promise when so many of his sons had died.

I explained to David everyone that had perished either betrayed or committed crimes against others in the family, so the Lord was doing as he had promised in keeping everyone safe. David thanked the Lord for allowing him to have the answer to his question as our procession moved slowly home to Jerusalem. David turned to me as if struck by a revelation.

"Moosie, do you realize I have spent almost no time in preparing Solomon to become king?" He said as we rode slowly toward Jerusalem.

I responded keeping my gaze to the road ahead, "Don't worry when the time comes he will prove worthy."

He turned to Joab and said, "Send word for the flags in the kingdom to be switched back over to my colors and raise them to full mast for our return."

Everyone came to cheer King David. The crowds waved and seemed happy their beloved king had returned safely home. Peace followed for a long time. My heart sang to be in Jerusalem once more.

Chapter Ten: Solomon's Coronation

As the tires screeched to a halt on the runway I became apprehensive. I had many questions I needed answered and hoped my contact possessed the answers. I stared out the plane window from my seat as if I would obtain immediate confirmation showing my dreams to be true to life. I finally arrived in Israel. A smile crept on my face as my thoughts went back to the campaigns across this land during a time when airports or highways did not exist. I smiled as I thought I witnessed this lands birth.

I grabbed my things and walked towards the door of the aircraft looking behind to make sure I didn't leave anything. My thoughts immediately went to the instructions via the note stuffed with my peanuts. It said to catch a cab to the address written down and then go to room 212. I moved to the baggage claim area, security seemed tight. A gentleman put his suitcase down and went to the water fountain only to get stopped two steps and told to take his property with him. The diligence of the Airport guards impressed me until a tap on my shoulder interrupted my thoughts. I turned around and a gentleman in a pair of dark sunglasses wearing a black leather jacket holding a loaded Uzi directed me to follow him.

"Sure." I said, as I followed behind him. He walked slowly gazing here and there around the Airport Terminal as if looking for someone or something. I started to gaze around as well because he was making me nervous. We got to a small room with a table and three chairs. There were no windows, pictures nor mirrors or anything on the dirty beige walls.

"Please, sit down." The security guard said.

"Why am I here? What did I do?" I asked as I sat in one of the brown wooden chairs placed around the table.

"My boss will explain when he arrives. Would you like some coffee?" he asked as he began to walk towards the door.

"No, I'm good." I responded.

He left the room and the door clicked. The door locked from the outside and could not be opened from the inside. I began to get nervous and wondered if coming here still seemed to be such a good idea. I shook my fear off and thought to myself how my whole life had been one struggle after the next. This was just the next I had to overcome. My leather clad jailer had only been gone for ten minutes when the door unlocked. He held a mug and sipped coffee, behind him an older man in a tailor made gray suit and rounded reading glasses carried a clipboard full of documents into the room.

"Why are you in Israel?" he asked, in a low voice.

"I came to tour Jerusalem and other holy sites" I responded in a higher tone attempting to get him to talk louder.

"Holy sites, which holy sites are you visiting?" He asked as he peered down at me over his glasses.

"I am here to pray at the Wailing Wall and." I hadn't finished answering the question when he went into another question.

"Where are you staying?" He asked me as he started walking towards the door.

"I will be staying at the Moriah Hotel in Tel Aviv." I almost told him the room number but I held my tongue because how would I know my room number if I hadn't checked in yet. He would definitely suspect something. He turned to the other man in the room whom had initially stopped me and said, "He is free to go." I immediately got up and went quickly back to the baggage claim where my bags still traveled around the rack. I grabbed them and left Ben Gurion International Airport with a bad feeling I would run into those guys again. I glanced over my shoulder as I exited the airport and headed towards the Taxi stand.

I took the time to unwind on the ride to the Hotel. I looked out of the window at the people and buildings hoping to recognize something or someone, but soon realized my loneliness. The butterflies in my stomach disappeared as I thought how the landscape had changed. Where stone and grass used to be now cement and glass stood. I then wondered had David or Solomon seen this time in their journeys as I had theirs. Everyone appeared to be preoccupied with life. Tel Aviv grew into a large city with so many buildings. I imagined the changes to Jerusalem probably matched what I witnessed here. As we pulled up to the Moriah the butterflies returned. I purposely moved slowly to pay the cabby. I was unsure of the next step and didn't want to rush into anything.

As I exited the elevator on the second floor it seemed my whole life flashed before me. I reflected on my dreams as I walked down this hall knowing the door at the end of it would probably change my life forever. My thoughts went back to David's time and to our return to Jerusalem. I dedicated myself to the task of readying Solomon for his duties as the heir. David and I were amazed at the speed in which Solomon grasped difficult concepts. In David's shadow Solomon had worked his way to second in line to rule behind Absalom. No one seemed to mind this gradual procession save for Adonijah, Solomon's older half brother. In the years following Absalom's civil war, Israel grew to become the most stable country in the region. The trade routes were protected, the borders were safe and the cities were garrisoned and thriving. David had nearly completed his task of compiling all the supplies necessary to build the temple.

David kept hinting to me how it was almost time for him to retire and pass the land to Solomon. He started to make plans for his retirement and the coronation of Solomon. Meanwhile Solomon's brother Adonijah had also received news of his father's wish to retire and rumors spread about how he began to prepare a coronation of his own, for himself. It seemed Adonijah understood outright warfare for the throne would be unsuccessful. Absalom had tried and failed. Adonijah would attempt to take the throne by political force. He secretly visited with the high ranking priests and community leaders within the country not knowing he was constantly being followed. He persuaded several priests to give him their loyalty and support, others he threatened or bribed. Many years had passed since the borders were initially secured. Joab had been assigned duties by David keeping him busy, but not actually commanding any units.

David had promoted a young tactician named Benaiah to second in command and who was now the actual day to day leader of Israel's military force under the command of Joab by rank only. It was mentioned to me by Solomon that Adonijah would possibly try to capitalize on the brushing aside of Joab and could play on his emotions to get Joab's support for him to take the throne instead of Solomon. Joab still had the loyalty of many and Adonijah's advisors later admitted he thought the mere threat of another civil war alone would be enough to cause David not to interfere with his non-violent assault on the throne.

I overheard a conversation as I went to visit Joab one day to tell him of my suspicions. As I got closer to the door a familiar voice came from the house, it was Adonijah's. I crept to the window to listen in.

"My dear nephew Joab, the land is preparing for change." Adonijah said in a half whisper.

Joab replied as he moved to sit his aging frame down on a workbench, "Adonijah I am too old and no longer a mover and shaker in the world of politics. Your father removed me from my old importance. Why do you bother me?"

Adonijah moved in closer and sat beside Joab as he said, "Joab, your name alone is all I need. No one would ask whether or not the troops were still loyal, for some are. My plans would not even go as far as fighting. With you by my side you will once again be Commander of the Force, Commander of a Force on the move, not sitting idle; rusting away!"

Joab's eyes seemed to glow at the thoughts of new battles and conquests. He said softly, "What would you need for me to do, simply attend your coronation?"

Adonijah's hand went to Joab's blue robed shoulder as he said, "Exactly; oh you might want to arrange security for the event as well. Can I count you in?"

Joab then held Adonijah's hands as he replied, "I'll be there, just make sure it goes well. Solomon may be passive now, but you may awaken a lion by trying to take from him what is his."

"Nothing is his, am I not a son of David? Then I too claim a birthright. Will you be there my dear nephew and commander?" Adonijah shouted as he walked toward the doorway heading straight for me.

"I will be there Adonijah." shouted Joab. I turned and hid along the side of the house until Adonijah had disappeared into the horizon and I visited with Joab as if nothing had happened. I later informed David and Solomon on what transpired. After Solomon left the throne room David turned to me and said, "Moosie, I do not want to put my people through another civil war."

With Joab's assistance and support Adonijah's plans were moving ahead better than he had originally imagined. David, Solomon and I kept up the appearances of our unawareness to his threat for the throne. The ever vigilant Bathsheba came to warn David. She told David Solomon's life may be in jeopardy. The depths of Adonijah's treachery were not known but support for him was gaining momentum throughout the priesthood. David swore to her he would put a stop to Adonijah's uprising.

David yelled into the corridor, "Guard, fetch Captain Benaiah and bring Solomon to me as well." Upon Benaiah and Solomon's arrival he promoted the young captain to Commander of the Force and made him swear allegiance to Solomon. "General Benaiah there is a plan afoot to steal Solomon's birthright. We shall outsmart these bandits without spilling any blood. Arrange for all the tribal leaders and priests of the land to gather on the morn of five days from now. Do not mention why they are being called to Jerusalem. Just tell them their King would like their presence."

Benaiah nodded and answered before turning to leave, "Yes my lord I shall make the arrangements immediately, and what of Joab?"

David scratched is grey beard as he answered, "He too is invited. Inform him and his legion of your promotion and his retirement before inviting him though."

Benaiah kneeled to one knee and said, "As you order my King."

General Benaiah accepted his blue robe as the Commander of the Force and departed to follow his orders. General Benaiah brought in troops loyal to him to secure Jerusalem for the Kings gathering. General Benaiah was a smart young tactician who had risen from the ranks of Absalom's divisions to become Absalom's second in command. Against the wishes of Joab he still used Absalom's standard colors as his own. David said he would allow this because it reminded him of Absalom and he did not wish to erase all memory of his son from the land. When Joab, the priests and the other tribal leaders arrived at the city to their surprise and Joab's dismay Absalom's colors were on all the guard towers flying underneath the King's colors. Joab's private and loyal units were moved to Elath and El Arish for this occasion. Only Joab's personal guard unit of five hundred men were at his immediate disposal.

This assured David, Benaiah and I that Joab would not be able to launch any attacks on this day. Adonijah seemed very nervous for he did not know why everyone was being gathered and his father so secretive. We made sure he noticed the change of guard so he would remain uneasy and off balance. We figured he would prefer the black and gold standards of Joab's guard on the watchtowers instead of our own. He had no reason to suspect we knew of his planned coupe. We sent out word this was just a gathering was for some tribute or monumental announcement of a new policy. It was actually the ceremony to coronate his brother Solomon, beating his own coronation by a month. As everyone gathered for the ceremony Adonijah moved through his supporters verifying their allegiances.

King David approached the audience. He was followed by Solomon, Benaiah and a few priests. Everyone grew silent to hear the king. "Hear me, my brethren, and my people; as for me, I had in mine heart to build a house of rest for the ark of the covenant of the Lord and for the footstool of our God, and had made ready for the building. But God said unto me, Thou shalt not build a house for my name, because thou hast been a man of war, and hast shed blood. Howbeit the Lord God of Israel chose me before all the house of my father to be king over Israel for ever; for he hath chosen Judah to be the ruler; and of the house of Judah, the house of my father; and among the sons of my father he liked me to make me king over all Israel."

"And all of my sons, (for the Lord has given me many sons) he hath chosen Solomon my son to sit upon the throne of the kingdom of the Lord over Israel. And he said unto me, Solomon thy son, he shall build my house and my courts: for I have chosen him to be my son and I will be his father. Moreover I will establish his kingdom forever, if he be constant to do my commandments and my judgments, as at this day. Now therefore, in the sight of all Israel the congregation of the Lord, and in the audience of our God, keep and seek for all the commandments of the Lord your God; that ye may possess this good land, and leave it for an inheritance for your children after you forever. And thou, Solomon my son, know thou the God of thy father, and serve him with a perfect heart and with a willing mind: for the Lord searcheth all hearts, and understandeth all the imaginations of thoughts: if thou seek him, he will be found of thee: but if thou forsake him, he will cast thee off forever."

"Take heed now; for the Lord hath chosen thee to build a house for the sanctuary: be strong, and do it…(**I Chronicles 28:02 – 28:10**) Upon the completion of Solomon's Coronation Adonijah crept away from the ceremony. All the people who had promised allegiance to Adonijah were leaving the ceremony except for Joab. The whole of the nation was at celebration because of the new King. The times of King David were now complete. King Solomon now reigned.

I sat for a moment wondering whether I was now a permanent fixture in this land. The Lord had brought me here; I have not aged a day since my arrival yet years and decades passed. I am honored for the Lord shows me favor and this experience I now live through or dream about will change me when I return to my time. I cannot be the same person. I know a tremendous amount and walked with King David, fought alongside Joab and now celebrate King Solomon's Coronation. I asked the Lord to show me my bloodline and my history and I am now immersed. I couldn't help to think this was building up to something. Everything happens for a reason. Perhaps I am being prepared for my time, my reign?

As I reached the door to room 212 my mind snapped back to the present as if it were being sucked in a vacuum. I paused a second before I knocked on the door. As I raised my hand to knock a voice from inside yelled, "It's Open." I slowly turned the doorknob and walked into the plush suite. An elderly man dressed in a blue suit like Matlock often wore sat at a table by a large window overlooking the Mediterranean. He gestured to the other seat on the other side of the table,

"Mustafa, welcome to Israel, please sit down." He said as he opened bottled water and poured it into a glass. I sat down opposite him at the table.

"May I ask your name, and for what reason you asked me here?" I said as I sat back in the chair preparing to finally learn the reason for my journey.

"You can call me Peter. We called you here to finally introduce ourselves to you." He said as he leaned forward in his chair and folded his hands on the table.

I looked around and replied, "We, who else is with you?"

He laughed as he shook his head in agreement, "Yes, we. I am a part of an organization formed centuries ago to protect you, your family and our religious beliefs from the dangers present in today's world. We call ourselves The British Israel World Federation or BIWF. We are called many names by different societies but throughout the centuries accomplished to protect religious artifacts with our methods. I will go into detail regarding our history sometime later."

"What makes my family so important?" I asked.

He stood up and walked towards the door making sure it was locked and dead bolted, "We believe you may be the heir to the throne of Israel. This may sound strange to you, but we intercepted government documents naming your family as being the heirs of King David."

I stood with my head reeling from what I had just learned, I had always suspected because of the dreams but never in a million years would think to ever have it confirmed by someone else. Why else would those dreams come to me? Everything was starting to make much more sense now. I regained my bearings and asked him, "What government documents?"

Peter walked over to the couch and sat down. He motioned for me to sit next to him and said, "As long as we can remember tyrants and governments searched for your family. Pharaoh tried to find your family and had all the babies killed but Moses survived. Herod hunted your family and conducted the slaughter of the innocents but Jesus survived. Hitler also scoured the earth for your family. He could not find them and killed hundreds of thousands yet I look upon your face now. He searched for your family's treasures all over the world and could not find what was hidden so long ago. After Israel was founded a protective shield formed in this country for your family's survival. We played a small part in attempting to place your family in a single part of the world where we could protect the Jewish population more effectively.

Creating Israel did not seem to help us or your enemies locate your family at all so scientists on both sides began DNA testing. They took samples from everything unearthed and compared those samples with today's living samples to find a match. Every chance allowed for a DNA test to be done on anyone is always taken. The DNA databank is vast. They tested bones believed to be of Jesus' relatives to those of King Tut. Everything is DNA tested and compared to the databank. Somewhere they obtained your DNA and it came up as a match and put you on a small list to be observed by the U.S. Government. We discovered these secrets as they were being disseminated throughout the Mossad hierarchy. That's where we first found your name."

"How long have you been watching me?" I asked in amazement.

He sat back on the couch and crossed his legs and explained, "We were drawn to you around fifteen years ago. The United States government actively prevents your, how can I say, your financial independence to keep you from being able to amass any wealth. We could not intervene until we were sure you were the true heir. When we discovered their campaigns against you it gave us confirmation and we sent you a ticket here."

I sat up on the couch and started firing questions at Peter, "So what are you saying, how did they stop my financial independence and what confirmation did you get? So you are sure I am the heir?"

Just then the phone rang. We both looked at each other as to wonder who else knew we were there. It rang a few times then stopped. Peter stood and walked to the door to check the peep hole, "Who did you tell you were here?"

I thought for a second then realized, "At the airport I told the security guys who held me."

Peter grabbed a beige trench coat from the closet and began unlocking the door. He turned before walking out and said, "I believe it is the Mossad, I am sure they are on their way up. What else did you tell them?"

I stood up from the couch and replied, "I just told them I was seeing the Holy sites."

"Well they are making sure you are here and no one is with you, someone will be knocking in a few I am sure of it. I will come by tomorrow morning. There is a lot to go over and much to do."

He shut the door quickly behind him. I walked over from the couch to see exactly which way Peter had gone, but by the time I went to reopen the door and look down the hall he disappeared. Two men in black leather jackets were walking towards me looking as if they needed to ask me something only to pass by me and use the exit to the stairs which I thought was weird since they had just walked off the elevator. Perhaps they got off on the wrong floor? I closed the door still taking in everything Peter had told me. I lied across the bed and forced myself to go back to the dream to the point where I spent my time with Solomon. I thought maybe if I reexamine my time with him it might help me to figure out what I was supposed to do here.

Chapter Eleven: The Return of the Prince of Egypt

I remembered Solomon ordered for the flags of his father David to continue to fly over Israel. As the future of Israel became Solomon's daily responsibility he prayed for the Lord's guidance every chance he got. David explained how the Lord would always bless the chosen heir before they wore the crown. Solomon understood David was not permitted to build the Temple because of his wars and of all the blood he had shed. He asked his priests not to allow him to become a warrior king so he could finish the Temple before anything occurred to place blood on his hands or threaten his ability to finish the task. He had hoped to complete the Temple while his father still lived, but just having his guidance to begin the process proved invaluable.

As I looked back at my time with David I thought of the exciting moments we shared. I wanted to know what my time with Solomon would be like and what adventures we would endure together. From the start of Solomon's reign peace ruled the land. We started many building projects throughout the kingdom. Solomon brought in several architects and named one to manage them all. The Chief Architect Jeroboam displayed his creativity and had lots of intriguing ideas. They became good friends over the years. Solomon wanted his legacy to live on in his buildings and monuments as the Egyptians did.

Meanwhile Solomon's spies reported they were not faring so well. Pharaoh after Pharaoh died from disease, scandal or rebellion. What we didn't know but soon found out was the current Pharaoh Siamun had a plan. A vision allowing him to strike at his enemies, fortify his borders as well as give him protection against rebellion. Kings and Pharaohs alike had heard of young King Solomon's coronation. The vast wealth, power, territory and security the Israelites now held did not escape the Egyptians attention.

Emissaries dispatched to Jerusalem from every kingdom near and far to get more information about this mighty King and to negotiate trade and treaties.

Solomon had learned well from David and Joab. He had placed spies everywhere and he would be an ally to the Pharaoh in more ways than one. Unaware of the Israeli spies in his Egyptian court, Pharaoh Siamun consulted with his advisors. This is the exchange King Solomon received as having occurred.

Pharaoh Siamun asked his advisors, "Tell me, a treaty with Israel would it be to my favor?"

The eldest advisor then stepped forward and replied, "Pharaoh Siamun, the Israelites carved out a huge kingdom and defend it well. They successfully isolated our outpost at Gezer so we cannot fortify or control the city. They are enjoying bountiful harvests and untold treasures. A pact with them would be most beneficial my Pharaoh"

The spies reported Pharaoh Siamun replied scratching his beard as he looked toward the horizon, "Egypt is suffering. I wish to stabilize this land to preserve our culture and my rule. An ally in Israel will strengthen my efforts. How do I secure this alliance?"

The eldest advisor stepped forward again and spoke softly almost in a whisper, "Lord Siamun, if we gave them Gezer as a gift, they would sign a pact."

"Would they? They are strong enough to take the city. How do we stop them? Would we wish to insult Israel by offering them something they are already in possession of?" replied Siamun.

"You are wise my lord, we would not want to stand against them right now." answered his advisor as he backed away from the Pharaoh.

"If I offer them the hand of my daughter Mehetemwaskhe; I could also offer them Gezer as a wedding gift. Pharaoh Siamun said rubbing his chin as if in deep thought. A pact would surely be accepted on those terms." he said as he gazed into the dark corners of his throne room."

"Pharaoh, you can not offer an outsider your daughter's hand. It is not our way. Since the beginning we never allowed a foreigner claim to the Egyptian throne." said his advisor sounding worried.

"Is King Solomon an outsider?" Siamun snapped, "Is not his ancestor Moses a Prince of Egypt sharing a Pharaohs home and obtaining a position in the court?" asked Siamun.

"Yes my Pharaoh, you are correct. Returning a Prince of Egypt would create a bond with Israel never to be broken. But my lord, what if they are blessed with a son?" as the advisor asked this question he backed away slowly.

Siamun responded laughingly, "We get ahead of ourselves. Let us present this proposition to King Solomon immediately."

Solomon's spies then reported Pharaoh Siamun sent his advisors to meet with Solomon. They told stories of how the Egyptian procession leaving for Jerusalem stretched for a mile long laden with gifts and gold. Pharaoh Siamun sent his personal guard to escort his daughter to Jerusalem. Upon reaching El Arish the procession halted as the Israeli Kingdom guards inquired about the reason for their appearance. The exchange by the Emissary with the kingdom guard as repeated to King Solomon went this way, "Brothers, we come offering gifts for his majesty the mighty King Solomon." The chief ambassador said.

The guard asked, "Where does this procession come from?"

"We are from the mighty and magnificent Pharaoh Siamun ruler of the Egyptian Empire. We come with gifts for his majesty King Solomon, may we pass?" replied the leader.

The Kingdom guard had already been alerted of their approach and allowed to give permission for entry. He responded, "Yes you may pass, but please stay on the major highway for your safety."

After the procession had passed the guard in charge of the El Arish post sent a messenger to his highness King Solomon informing him of the approaching Egyptian procession's entrance into the kingdom. When King Solomon learned of the oncoming procession he called in his advisors and I to consult with.

"Gentlemen, approaching us is a procession from Pharaoh Siamun bearing gifts. What does he possibly want in return for the gifts he brings? We all heard the news from our spies so would this simply be for a nonaggression pact?" Solomon asked looking directly at me for which I assumed he meant for me to answer.

Instead the chief advisor responded, "My lord, I am certain all he wants is to arrange a peace accord. His country is in turmoil and he needs the strength and wisdom of your crown to sustain his reign."

Solomon responded, "The Egyptians do not usually offer marriage to anyone outside the royal family. Why would they offer this to me and should I accept this offer?"

"My lord, you are royalty, as reported by the spy. Your great-great grandfather Moses had been raised in the Pharaoh's own home. He held the title of a Prince of Egypt at one time." The chief advisor responded.

"This is true. Do you believe they wish to restore that title to me? Call my father to me I will consult with him as well." Solomon said taking a seat on the throne looking bewildered.

His advisors left and went to retrieve and brief David of the events. "Solomon you sent for an old King?" David asked as he slowly walked into the throne room.

"Father, an Egyptian procession is approaching bearing gifts for me." Solomon told his father as he sat heavily on the throne.

"Solomon, this is outstanding. Whatever they offer, whatever they want, take it. The Egyptians watch on high all the lower kingdoms. They believe themselves to be more prominent than any other kingdom. For them to accept us as a kingdom and offer you a treaty is quite the accomplishment." David said smiling and placing his aged hand upon Solomon's purple velvet caped shoulder.

"Father they also bring with them a bride. She is a princess for me to wed." Solomon said standing up and walking towards a throne room window overlooking his palace grounds.

"Oh, Solomon this is most blessed news" Exclaimed David, "This will make you a Prince of Egypt with a claim to the Egyptian throne!"

"Yes, this I know. Pharaoh Siamun might be placing me right in the middle of a Civil War where I would be bound to fight for him as a son in marriage?" Solomon asked David as he sat on the throne as if a heavy weight had been placed on his shoulders.

"My son, I do not know what this Pharaoh is contemplating, but you must do what you believe is right for this Kingdom. Your claim to the Egyptian throne does not hold you responsible for Egyptian affairs. You must always remember your responsibilities to our own people and the Temple you must construct. Your hands cannot become bloody for the Egyptians or anyone else. Always know the power of a treaty. Treatises are more profitable than combat, they give you more in return and come at less expense." Said David, "Mustafa, you should remember this advice as well." David added as he glanced in my direction. I shook my head yes to show my agreement.

"I understand father. Thank you for your words." Solomon answered as he bowed while David shuffled slowly from the brightly lit Chamber.

When the procession reached Jerusalem Solomon graciously accepted Pharaoh Siamun's offer. Egyptian law made it uncommon for an Egyptian princess to wed outside of her immediate family so the offer honored him. Gezer, the last Egyptian outpost now landlocked behind the borders of Solomon's kingdom had been offered as well. The Egyptians barely held on to the territory and we were glad to get the last piece of occupied land within our borders and fortified the city immediately.

After the pact Solomon and I often visited and counseled with Pharaoh Siamun. David and I still chatted daily and he commented how proud he was of his son becoming more of a diplomat than he had ever been. Solomon had already managed to control Gezer through diplomatic means, a city in which neither David nor any of his Generals ever conquered. The Philistines whom still controlled many cities near Gezer swore they would retake the city once the chance arose. Upon hearing those threats Solomon immediately ordered for the refortification of all the cities walls and defenses. He also tripled the guard in each city. Solomon appeased the Philistinian King by giving him a gift of tremendous gold and jewels in payment for Gezer. An uneasy peace followed for decades.

One night God visited Solomon in a dream. Solomon had told me The Lord had shown him, as he had shown David the future of his kingdom as well as his rightful and righteous heirs to the throne throughout time. It made Solomon proud to know his blood remained precious to the Lord. In a dream the Lord asked, *"Solomon, what gift am I to bestow upon a King?"* Solomon realized this question disguised a riddle. What practical and precious gift would a King want to be given?

He explained how he wanted a gift not only useable by him, but something his bloodline benefitted from far into the future. Riches are too easily spent, power is too fleeting and long life would doom him to walk the earth for longer than he probably would care for as friends, family and loved ones died around him. Wisdom, yes it would be wisdom. Unparalleled wisdom would be requested, wisdom to flow from him to the rightful and chosen heirs of Israel throughout time. He went on to tell how in the dream the Lord, impressed by his request granted it to be binding forever. This is what enabled me to visit. The Lord gave Solomon the ability to understand the truth. His knowledge and insight knew no boundaries and were unmatched by any human. He was also given the ability to see good and evil whenever it was present.

In this dream the Lord told Solomon, *"Your kingdom will shine brighter than any the world will ever know. Your wisdom will be legendary my son, and your blood is sacred and protected."* Solomon told me he arose the next morning wiser than most men. He ordered for his flag to be designed. Solomon had received the idea for his flag from his conversations in his dreams with the Lord. His flag would be the flag of his father save for lines protruding from the spaces around the star. His standards would transform the Star of David into the shining Star of Solomon to represent the brightness of his kingdom throughout time. His seamstresses began work immediately on the new flag of their king. This flag would fly over the Temple once completed. Not long after the completion of Solomon's banner, his father died. Solomon and I grieved and found no comfort. His most experienced counselor and my dearest friend had passed. He ordered his fathers flags to be flown at half mast for thirty days to mourn the great king. Upon the end of the thirty days Solomon's new flags flew high in every city and fortification in the land of Israel.

Chapter Twelve: Makeda

The next morning was beautiful; I awoke well rested to singing birds, open curtains and the sun shining brightly into my hotel room. A knock at the door startled me as I brushed my teeth. I opened the door to a smiling female face.

"Room service sir, here is your breakfast, coffee and orange juice." She said with a large smile.

I didn't want to tell her she had the wrong room, so I took the meal anyway. Whose ever breakfast this happened to be came right on time because I was starving. I began to tear into the food when another knock at the door broke the sound of munching and crunching. I started to get frustrated with all the disturbances. I opened the door half expecting the young woman whom delivered my meal asking if I had already begun eating. Instead the stern and elderly face of Peter greeted me. He didn't wait for me to invite him in, he quickly brushed past me.

"Morning Mustafa, You ate yet? Is my coffee here as well? Ah yes." He said as he began mixing cream and sugar into the cup.

"Eat up my boy there is much to go over. Yesterday we just touched the tip of the iceberg." He said taking a seat on the couch as if to get ready for a long tale.

"Where should I begin?" He said as he scratched his head while he fiddled for something in his beige trench coat.

I took a bite into my toast and said, "How about if I ask you a question and you answer? Perhaps this will get the ball rolling."

He pulled a pipe from his pocket and placed the old worn object in his mouth, "Fire away then."

"Who am I, what is happening to me and why should I trust you?" I asked as I moved across the room and sat on the edge of the bed.

Peter sat back on the couch and took several puffs of the pipe. "Well Mustafa this goes back as far as David and to the promise in which God made to him. He promised his family would always rule Israel and be blessed and protected by him. Since God's promise Satan and those who would conspire with him attempt to do everything in the world to discredit the Lord and to destroy your family."

"Through histories attempts to destroy your family, you survive. The Lord keeps you quite safe. Who you are is simple. You are not Jesus. You are simply of the bloodline in which he is to be born...if he is to be born again. Many believe he will descend from the heavens. Many believe he will be born again unto man. Your death and the death of those who would come after you would prevent his return as it pertains to a normal birth. Many do not wish the messiahs return at all. The agents of Satan will stop at nothing to kill you and your family."

"I hope this explains who we believe you are, now as to what is happening. When we discovered you, if you remember from yesterday I told you we intercepted a document from the Mossad naming your family and most of all you as being the heir to the kingdom of Israel. We obtained the information but several of our comrades lost their lives while inflicting grave damages to the Mossad. Since your discovery we continued tracking you and attempted to thwart every plan to bug your phones, crash your computer or even deny you credit. Our efforts have not gone unnoticed. Our covert operations to protect you triggered panic amongst an unknown enemy. We believe they actually think you might be the messiah resurrected or the catalyst to Armageddon somehow. You may actually be the welcoming party to the actual Messiah, sort of like the Joseph of our time if you will. We are sure the Mossad or the Americans are not trying to kill you because you wouldn't have been allowed out of America or into Israel. We are still determining where the threat is originating from."

I cut Peter short, "This is all crazy." I said, "This is too much."

"Do you deny being related to King David?" Peter said, looking at me through his bifocals as if to burn a hole into my soul.

"I won't deny or confirm anything." I said standing up from the table. "Your organization is placing my life in danger."

Peter looked down at the carpet as he responded, "I deeply apologize. We realized this fact and called you here. We offer to send you deeper into hiding for your protection by providing you a new identity and offering you even greater protection until we can figure out what is happening."

I walked to the window as I took in everything presented to me this morning. "Peter, give me some time please. This is a lot of information to take in."

Peter immediately got up, "Sure thing Mustafa, take as much time as you need. I will check in on you tomorrow morning ok?" As he walked out I locked all the locks and deadbolts. I suddenly became quite afraid. My mind reeled. I found myself on my knees to pray for the Lords guidance and smiled to myself as I remembered Solomon and David spent much of their time on their knees. I finally understood why they stayed on their knees. I began to cry as I asked the Lord to guide me for I knew not where I headed.

What would the Lord want me to do here in Israel? The question haunted my thoughts. To find solace I took my mind back to Solomon and remembered our experiences together. I went back to a time with Solomon when the Temple was close to completion. Solomon spent most of his time tending to the daily duties of running his vast kingdom. Fortifying cities with newly constructed walls and adding castles seemed to be his passion. Megiddo had been fortified during this time along with El Arish, Eilat and many other cities. He also completed one of the most splendid throne rooms in the world. A throne of Solid Gold, Ivory and Burgundy Silk Tapestry sat atop thirteen cream colored Marble steps protected by thirteen golden lions on the side of each step representing the thirteen tribes of Judah.

Adonijah silently watched his brother become the greatest king in the world as he completed the Temple. Rumors of how he never stopped thinking of other ways in which he could ascend to the throne spread throughout the kingdom. Solomon had spared his life once already and told him any more attempts would not be treated as kindly. Meanwhile Jerusalem thrived and upon the completion of the Temple had become the largest trading center in the region. Merchants from all over the world came to Jerusalem because of Solomon's wealth.

The day of the Temple's completion Solomon ran to my chambers and burst through the door yelling, "Moosie, the Temple is finished. Quick come look. I have never been as happy as I am today and my only disappointment is my father cannot be here."

I arose from my bed tripping over my shoes hurrying to got dressed as I replied, "Solomon he is proud of you."

Solomon drank wine for the first time since his placement upon the throne and he reveled for an entire month in celebration of its completion. During the month of celebration Mehetemwaskhe informed him of her pregnancy. She had not begun to show, but had missed her cycle. The happiness we saw on Solomon's face to be a father as well as finish the Temple overwhelmed everyone. The Lord had blessed him truly. We celebrated for the entire month and every year thereafter held celebrations honoring the completion the Temple. I felt it no coincidence this celebration occurred in December.

Several months had gone by and many visitors had come and gone to visit the completed Temple. One day a visitor dressed in glorious silken robes came into the throne room to announce someone who travelled extreme distances to sit with the king. Solomon agreed to sit with the traveler and told them to announce the visitor.

The aide shouted in a loud voice gesturing with open arms to the door, "Introducing Makeda, The Queen of Sheba." Everyone's eyes focused on the door and the throne room grew silent as the most beautiful woman I ever seen entered. Her skin was a flawless even toned dark brown complexion highlighted by trace amounts of makeup. You could tell by the expression on Solomon's face he also shared the same thoughts as I did. Makeda approached Solomon's throne with many gifts of gold, silver and animal furs from her Kingdom in Nubia. The two spent many hours together talking and comparing notes about their respective kingdoms.

Mehetemwaskhe did not like the lack of attention she now received from her husband and displayed her dislike publicly. She often asked guards or advisors about the time Solomon spent with Makeda.

One afternoon while walking the garden path with Solomon I whispered, "Solomon, Mehetemwaskhe is asking everyone questions about you and Makeda. She is far along in her pregnancy and I believe she is starting to become self conscious about her looks."

Solomon gave me a puzzled look and replied, "She is beautiful, why is she worried?"

I sat down on a step and rubbed my head wondering how I could put this in a way as to not offend him, "Solomon, Mehetemwaskhe might think she cannot compete with the beautiful Makeda. The rumors are getting vicious."

Solomon had heard the rumors as well. He sat down beside me and replied, "Moosie, the truth is Mehetemwaskhe despises Makeda. I believe she hates Makeda not only because of her apparent beauty, but because of her wisdom as well. Being the daughter of a Pharaoh and my wife is as elegant as a woman could be. Why does she hate Makeda so?"

"Solomon she holds everything except one thing." I said.

He turned to face me with his eyebrows raised and said, "What is that?"

I laughed and replied, "Power."

"Moosie" Solomon said to me as he arose from the step and walked into the throne room where he gazed out an open window, "I cannot look upon this jealousy from Mehetemwaskhe towards Makeda any longer than I must. After she gives birth I will send her to El Arish with Jeroboam who will build her a palace."

I walked towards Solomon, "Yes but her jealousy will not be eased. Spend some time with her before she departs. I am only thirteen and my experience with women is limited but my mother and father never spent time together as many people often asked them to. Perhaps if you spend time with her she will understand her importance in your life."

"You give me wise advice. You are becoming good counsel to me. I am thankful for your visit." Solomon said as he turned and faced me, "I will go to her and bring my child into a loving world."

As Solomon left, my thoughts went to my mom, dad and even my sisters. I missed them greatly and wanted to go home. I had been in this continuous dream for what seemed like eons. I giggled as I thought of Dorothy in the Wizard of Oz. I didn't want to panic I understood God would send me home in time. Months later Mehetemwaskhe gave birth to a son. Solomon named his firstborn with Mehetemwaskhe, Nemrat.

Nemrat seemed strong from birth, he had royal blood coursing through his veins. He is a prince of princes; a Prince of Egypt and the Prince to the throne of Israel. With Mehetemwaskhe now busy with their newborn son and preparing for her journey to El Arish, Solomon had much more time to spend alone with his new love Makeda. Solomon and Makeda seemed to be falling deep in love with each other. One afternoon while sitting in the King's courtyard I overheard Makeda and Solomon.

Solomon spoke to Makeda, his voice full of concern, "Makeda why are you so distant, what is the matter my love? In such a short time you have become a vital part of my life. If you pain I do as well. Why does your face hold such sorrow?"

Makeda sighed gently and begun to talk in her beautiful melodious African accented voice, "Solomon, please sit with me. My time with you is a walk through the clouds. I never learned so much or loved anyone as much as I love you. I wish I could spend all my days here by your side."

Solomon broke in, "You can, stay with me forever."

Makeda cut him off politely, "Solomon wait. This is extremely hard for me so please let me finish. I am a Queen, I must return to rule my people and conduct the affairs of my country lest my enemies find me absent and scourge over my land. My heart is yours, my religion is yours, and my child is also yours."

Solomon interrupted as I almost fell off the bench, "Your child?"

Makeda responded, "Yes, my child is yours as well my love."

Solomon sounded extremely excited, "Makeda this is the greatest of news! A strong son I am sure. We will hold our tongues and keep this betweenst us for now."

Makeda swiftly responded, "I agree, I must depart soon as travel will become difficult for me. I leave you with a heavy heart but I will forever have a piece of you with me."

I stood and walked around the corner while Solomon embraced her and said, "I will visit once you send word for me."

Makeda spent several more weeks with us. When she finally left Jerusalem, only a few of us knew she left bearing Solomon's unborn child. He promised we would visit her kingdom and experience the jungle he had heard so much about, but had never before seen. After Makeda's departure Jeroboam returned from Cairo where he studied their building techniques. Solomon sent Mehetemwaskhe and Nemrat to El Arish with Jeroboam and charged him with constructing a grand fortress. Nemrat grew up near his Egyptian grandfather Pharaoh Siamun in El Arish. Solomon wanted Siamun to instruct Nemrat on the ways of a Pharaoh.

Chapter Thirteen: The Grand Embarkations

Years had passed since Makeda's visit. She had a strong son for Solomon and he had travelled many times to sit with Solomon. Sometime after he turned thirteen Solomon and I planned to go to his home and welcome him into manhood.

During this time of happiness in Solomon's life Adonijah made his last play for the throne. Bathsheba came into the throne room and spoke with Solomon, "Son, your brother Adonijah asked me to speak with you regarding him marrying Mehetemwaskhe. Adonijah said one old wife far away shouldn't be a problem to give to him when there are so many others to comfort you."

Solomon reached for and held his mother's hand, "Mother, I will take this request under advisement since it falls from your lips."

Bathsheba smiled and waved to me as she walked out. As soon as she left the throne room he called for General Benaiah.

"Benaiah, my brother Adonijah is attempting another move for the throne." snapped Solomon, obviously livid over this new betrayal.

"What would you wish for me to do my Lord?" asked Benaiah.

Solomon moved closer to the General and whispered as if ashamed to give the order, "Kill Adonijah and whomever else you believe is involved with this!" he then began to yell, "Now the Temple is built shall my enemies force my hands to be stained with blood? I will never again be responsible for the death of anyone whom does not present a clear and present danger to my rule. I will not become the animal my father warned me of."

Benaiah left the throne room to follow through on his orders. Solomon gazed over at me and said, "Moosie this is the perfect time to visit my son and Makeda."

"I agree my King I would love to visit with the Queen. A safari would be nice." I responded. In the back of my mind I wondered if the blank check kill order he just gave led Benaiah to believe he had cause to settle old scores.

Solomon walked over to the table and sat beside me, "This trip will be more than a safari. The Lord instructed me to prepare hiding places for my treasures. As well as spread his name to the four corners of the earth. Before we take this trip to Makeda I must prepare four voyages to spread my religion and my name. On the way to Makeda I must find a place to hide my most beloved of treasures for," He did not finish.

I immediately asked, "For what Solomon?"

He moved a bit closer to me and said, "For your time. You must remember where we hide the treasures. You will need them. The parties I must send out are all for the future. They are my gifts to you for what you give to my father and I. The treasures each party carries may be of some use to you once you locate their final destinations."

I stood and bowed as I said, "Thank you Solomon, right now I don't exactly know of what you speak, but I am sure you do. I am even surer I will wish to thank you again in my time. So I will take the time here to thank you."

It took us a few years to prepare for the trip and come up with a suitable route. During our preparation Solomon took a visit by his son Nemrat who turned sixteen. He told his father how he had been a part of Pharaoh Siamun's conquest of the southern tribes with the help of King Milesius. Milesius ruled Spain and also married one of Siamun's daughters. Solomon and Milesius had become close over the years and he treated Nemrat as his own son. Nemrat also told Solomon he planned on returning with Milesius to fight the Libyans and then sail with Milesius to a new land he was preparing to conquer. This seemed to spark Solomon's interest.

He stared at the ceiling of the throne room as he spoke to Nemrat, "This new land he prepares to conquer. He will attack it by sea?"

Nemrat sat on the marble step and answered, "Yes, we will travel through the mouth to open seas and then move up for seven days to this land."

Solomon scratched his head as if deep in thought and said, "I would like to send a landing party with this force if I may. I will dispatch a messenger to Milesius.

Nemrat quickly answered, "There is no need father, I am in command of a legion that will travel with Milesius. You can send the party with me I will make sure they reach their destination safely."

Solomon rubbed Nemrat's head and replied, "They shall not return son. They are there to set up a colony and spread the word of my lord and tell everyone of Jerusalem for all the days to come."

Nemrat stood and said, "I understand, I will send word exactly one month from the time we are to depart. This should allow time for your party to sail out and meet us."

Nemrat's mood then turned serious as he spoke, "Father, it is with a heavy heart I report the indecencies of Jeroboam and my mother."

Solomon fell back deeper into his throne and seemed deflated as he said, "What are you reporting my son?"

Nemrat went to one knee on the step in front of his father and said, "He stays with her into the nights and keeps her company during the days. Something is bothering her. Please give her a visit."

Solomon stood, bowed low and said, "I thank you commander Nemrat be safe and victorious."

A few months later Solomon dispatched his four emissary parties. Each party travelled with five thousand people and enough food for them to last two years. Solomon told the crew of each vessel to sail until they found land and instructed the lead ambassador to travel twelve moons into the land and create a settlement once they landed. They had to spread the word of The Lord to whomever they met and tell all of Solomon, his wisdom and his kingdom. The ships were larger than any I had ever seen. His ships were captained by hardy seaman from surrounding lands who would return scouts to Solomon with news of the settlement locations and bring back animals or anything else of value from their expedition.

Two parties left from El Arish and travelled west, the other two parties left from Eilat and travelled east. I never knew what treasures were taken with each party and Solomon made sure I had nothing to do with helping them load the ships. As we watched the ships depart from El Arish I marveled at how large the sails were. They had a light blue background with a shining gold star emblazoned directly in the center.

Solomon pointed and said, "The flying carpets of Solomon shall bring speed to those vessels."

I laughed as the ships sailed off with their sails full of air. I took a double glance because the ships did appear as if they were being carried away by large carpets. I did not know until years later I had witnessed the world's first sight of the sail. Solomon's flying carpets became the hottest topic in every kingdom around the globe. We travelled back to Jerusalem to prepare for our upcoming journey. Even though we were to travel with a hundred thousand soldiers and twenty thousand servants we both understood we could lose many to disease or other disasters. We began our long journey on a rainy morning in Jerusalem and travelled southwest towards El Arish where we would visit Mehetemwaskhe before we moved south to sit with Siamun.

The uneventful and slow journey to El Arish allowed Solomon to concentrate on his people. Mothers and children waved and sang as Solomon moved along the sandy roads through their towns. He waved back and sang aloud with them; thus the reason the people loved him. I watched his interaction with them and thought how I must take in everything I can from him as I did with David. The Israeli countryside was beautiful and peaceful. I would have been safe traveling these roads alone. David had made the borders of this new world power respected by all whom had dealings with him in the past. I thought of all I had seen and done since I had arrived here. This story I must remember, who would believe such a journey took place? I learned so much in what Solomon referred to as my Bar Mitzvah. I smiled as I thought how much of a man I would return home as. I whispered so only Falazel could hear me, "What does the road hold before us old friend, what does it hold?"

We finally reached El Arish. I had been to the city on various occasions and the beauty of the city overwhelmed me every time I visited. The palm trees stood majestically under the light blue cloudless sky and the weather was always lovely. The winter always amazed me here because the temperature could be seventy-five degrees and there would be a cool wind whipping over the Mediterranean from Europe. You could actually feel Europe's winter on the wind yet the warmth of the sun made the breeze refreshing instead of cold. The castle walls glistened like marble in the sun and most of the views overlooked the Mediterranean. Jeroboam did an excellent job on the city. Only Solomon's personal guard and I followed into the courtyard of the palace where Mehetemwaskhe waited.

Solomon hopped from his white horse smiling as he went to embrace his lovely wife, "Mehetemwaskhe, you are even lovelier than my dreams remembered. How are you my love?"

She was happy to see him, but seemed to have something weighing on her mind as she returned his embrace, "Solomon, I am fine, I just miss you and Nemrat is away in Libya under constant attack. I am just heavy hearted in my loneliness"

As if on cue Jeroboam walked from the castle and waved to Solomon as he said, "My lord I did not know you were to grace us with your presence today. I am checking on some last minute details to reinforce the walls."

Solomon did not seem amused at Jeroboam coming from the chambers and replied, "Wall reinforcements, thank you Jeroboam you are always working tediously for the king."

Solomon returned his attentions back to his wife and gently placed his hand behind her neck and said to her as he gazed into her eyes, "My love you will not be lonely tonight, nor tomorrow or the night after. Would you travel to sit with your father when we leave?"

She began to cry as she buried her head into Solomon's chest and said, "Yes, I will go with you, I would follow you anywhere, let us retire."

We spent the next few days in El Arish enjoying the beach, food and trade until it was time to hit the road for Tanis. Tanis was not far from El Arish, only about a ten days ride along the shores. Siamun was always especially happy to see Solomon and I. We sat with Siamun and talked of all things from A to Z before moving onwards towards Sana'a to visit Makeda and Menelik. Siamun seemed apprehensive and anxious to discuss plans for the kingdom upon his death for some reason.

Siamun waved for Solomon to sit next to him. After Solomon sat Siamun leaned over and said, "Solomon, I am sure my enemies are close and my days are numbered here."

Solomon's face turned deathly serious as he replied, "Siamun point in the direction of any trouble and all Israel is emptied to protect you and I am even surer all Gaul would empty as well."

Siamun patted Solomon on the knee as he laughed and said, "Solomon do not trouble over the affairs of an old Pharaoh. You have your travels through dangerous enemy territory to worry about, besides I will put up a good enough fight. Should I fall, promise me you will help Nemrat sit on this throne. I know this is much to ask, for if he sits here he cannot rule Israel but you are blessed with hordes of sons."

Solomon cut him short, "Pharaoh Siamun you indeed ask much of me, but I know my heir and Nemrat is not he. If anything should happen to you I will make sure Nemrat takes your throne even if I must lead the march against your enemies alone."

Siamun smiled and placed his hand upon Solomon's shoulder and said, "Thank you Solomon. Nemrat's safety is a concern of mine as well. I doubled his guard and sent him from the castle on raids. He will be safer on the foreign battlefields with Milesius and his sons."

Solomon smiled back as he replied, "Lord Siamun I thank you for your kindness and for the protection of my son. You will destroy your enemies and I will sit with you upon my return from this vast jungle I am about to enter."

Siamun grasped Solomon's hand and replied, "Bring me a Lions pelt, I always wanted one but never went to obtain one for myself."

Solomon laughed a loud hearty laugh and responded, "I will try hard to get what you asked for. A Lion is a handful and may get the best of me, but I will die trying. Goodbye Pharaoh Siamun."

We turned and left Pharaoh Siamun's throne room for the black waters of the Nile. The Pharaoh had prepared a large flotilla fully supplied for our trip. They awaited our arrival at the staging area in Fayum. When we arrived boats covered the entire water. You could barely lay eyes on the water there were so many boats. Solomon sent word for his grand navy to set sail down the Red Sea. He wanted them to meet us near Sana'a after his visit with Makeda. He ordered for everything written on a list he handed to the messenger to be loaded on the ships and taken with them. I did not read the paper but something told me I would know first hand all the things on it real soon.

Chapter Fourteen: Into the Dense Jungles of Africa

We started our voyage into the darkness of Africa with little fanfare. On the initial leg of the trip we floated down the Nile past Hippopotamus and Crocodile. I wished I had been equipped with a camera, because no one would believe this. The Nile flowed pure, everyone still drank from it. We visited the cities along the banks whenever possible. Trading for exotic animals, spices and gems excited Solomon and led to his mystique as he spent tons of gold to acquire almost everything the traders put in front of him. While we visited a city near Aswan a messenger caught up to us with the most horrifying news.

He informed Solomon of Pharaoh Siamun's untimely death and the rise to power of a Pharaoh named Psusennes. Solomon immediately expected foul play and sent word to Nemrat who now fought with Milesius' army on an Island now known as Ireland. His message told Nemrat to hold his hand until Solomon returned home. He also wanted to know the exact location of the landing parties' settlement in Ireland.

We boarded a little more apprehensive because the next leg of the trip began the danger as we travelled up the Nile into the Nubian countries making our way to the third cataract. Night came swiftly on the Nile and in the night strange sounds surrounded us in the pitch blackness of Africa. Solomon wanted to keep the flotilla lightless so enemies would not be able to track the group. Every now and again a fire covered arrow would fly from the trees and land in the river missing the boats. They tried to light us up to monitor our progress on the river. We awoke to a completely different scene.

The desert no longer ruled, instead thick vegetation filled the banks of the Nile. The jungle was so thick you could not see much farther than the coastline. Children and women ran along the beaches trying to keep pace with us. The guards seemed a little unsettled until Solomon told them to be at ease. He told me, "We are in no danger. No man would put his women and children in danger. If the women and children disappear, then you need to worry."

I made sure I kept seeing little figures and women on the coast to ease my fears. Solomon said to me, "Any way we should be safe until we hit around the fifth cataract. Our guard will have to be up and we will pick up speed as a group."

I asked Solomon with fear in my voice, "How do we know when we reach the fifth cataract?"

Solomon smiled at me and said, "Oh I think we will have an idea when to pick up the pace."

I sat uneasily in the dark and looked all around when I noticed a figure move swiftly behind one tree and run to another. I had been through plenty of battles now and had been saved any pain in them. I didn't want this to be my end by taking an errant arrow only to wake up in my pajamas back in Philly. Solomon spread the word how we would travel. We rowed full speed at night and half speed while alternating sleep during the day. The sun had not quite risen and I gazed into the trees on the banks when I was startled out of my skin by Solomon's booming voice, "Row quickly. Row and don't stop until the sun is high."

Our oarsmen began to row. I had never seen anything like this before. We moved on the river faster than I thought possible and amazingly we didn't pull away from anyone. We had gone about a mile when in the distance the booming of drums could be heard. They grew louder and louder as we travelled south. Benaiah screamed, "Shields up, protect the king fire at anything on the banks. We must be silent and fast!" After he gave the order and not a moment sooner the air grew black with arrows from the trees.

"Watch out!" I screamed as I grabbed my shield, fell to the bottom of the boat and cowered under the large piece of iron.

"Moosie, get smaller under your shield and don't move until you feel the boat slow down." Solomon yelled above the drums.

"I am too young to die Solomon and I can't swim!" I replied.

"Me too!!" he jokingly yelled back.

A sense of humor under these conditions I thought to myself. Benaiah barked commands to his men to keep the oars manned and to throw the dead overboard. We travelled what seemed like forever under fire. I fell asleep and awoke sometime later with the boat still moving swiftly but everything had turned dark again and grew chillingly silent. I remembered Benaiah said we were to be quiet once the night fell and everyone complied. I stayed buried under my shield and went back to an uneasy sleep.

The next morning I awoke to a still boat tied up on the shores of the river. I jumped up immediately and looked for Solomon when I found him on the banks looking at a map. I went to him and asked, "Where are we?"

He pointed at the map and said, "Well good morning Moosie, we have crossed into the White Nile and are several leagues ahead of our pursuers. We have stopped to gather our bearings and take care of the wounded. We will leave in a few minutes."

I smiled and replied, "I will be in the boat."

The heat bothered me and made me ready to start moving so our (pursuers) didn't catch up with us. Solomon promptly returned to the boat and we once again began our journey up the Nile. We travelled for most of the day with the men and I reaching into the Nile and splashing water onto our bodies to keep cool. Solomon seemed relieved as he said, "We are almost to the land part of our travel. Advance scouts have returned with a perfect place for me to bury my treasures until you can recover them in your time."

I replied, "How long before we reach land?"

Solomon glanced up at the sky and towards the banks and said, "Fifteen more sun rises."

He stood up and said, "We need to pick up a little more speed we seem to have picked up enemy scouts."

I turned towards the banks and five figures ran behind us just inside the tree line. I responded, "Can they run with us the whole time?"

Solomon laughed as he said, "I guess we are going to find out."

We continued up the Nile for what seemed liked months. The scenery didn't change much and the sun had no mercy on our skin. The river soothed, but we had to continuously reach into the river and pour water over our heads to stay cool. This in itself became dangerous because the river was infested with crocodiles and we had already lost many men to the river croc as they became careless. On the day we reached the big lake which is now called Lake Victoria a big horn from the front of the procession sounded. Solomon turned and said, "We have arrived!" The river opened up into a large lake. At first I thought we had dumped into the ocean and I became nervous because of the size of our boats, but soon realized it was a lake and we moved toward the farthest shore.

We pulled into a Kenyan city named Kibara where we met with our land procession from Queen Makeda already prepared and ready for our arrival. Makeda had made sure we received protection. She sent what seemed like no less than five hundred thousand warriors to guide us back to her kingdom. Traveling with a force such as this made me more at ease than the river leg of the journey. I turned around to see if we still had pursuers within sight. Only the warriors from Makeda and Solomon's personal guard followed. We crossed into the Serengeti and the wildlife thrilled everyone. In the distance a mighty roar froze Solomon and I in our tracks. Solomon grabbed me with excitement and said, "What was that?"

I smiled and said, "My dear Solomon that would be your Lion."

Solomon sighed, "Siamun is dead, but I did promise him a Lion kill." He blew his horn and yelled, "Hold the procession!" He called for his personal guard and Makeda's General to help him go after his Lion. I stayed behind, I wanted to take in the sights and catch up on my sleep. I had not gotten much sleep on the Nile and chose to catch up here in the peace and calm of the Serengeti. Several hours had passed when Solomon returned excited and stained with blood and mud from head to toe. We did not talk of his hunt when he returned. He cleaned himself of the blood and went to sleep. Upon awaking from his nap we immediately resumed our journey through Kenya. We left the plains and slowly ascended into the mountain ranges of the country.

He turned to me, "Moosie, I think we are close to where the treasure can be hidden. I would like to hide it within a mountain top, high above the land where the average person cannot reach."

The guide turned and said, "We come to highest mountain in land soon."

Solomon replied, "This is where we will go. Lead us."

The heat prevailed at night and the heat ruled during the day here in Africa. Every day seemed hotter than the next. We descended a mountain range and in the distance our destination beckoned to us. The mountain in front of us was huge, terribly high and covered with snow. Solomon had seen snow for the first time on the mountain we currently came down from and I had shown him the wonders of ice, cold water, meat preservation and snowballs of course. We came to a rock formation resembling a half moon. Solomon said, "Moosie this will be where you will begin your journey to the treasure. I will leave clues from here for you to follow to the summit of the mountain."

He turned to Benaiah and said, "This is where the treasure will rest, the summit of the mountain will do nicely. Prepare the site and be sure to use plenty of traps for looters."

Benaiah responded, "Yes my lord we shall begin our work immediately."

Solomon said, "I will return with the treasures to be placed within the hold. They await me at sea."

Benaiah bowed and said, "The project will be ready upon your return my lord, I trust your safety with Makeda's General I will stay here and oversee the work."

We left General Benaiah with everyone except a handful of the original procession. We continued onward with Makeda's warriors into the jungles of Africa.

Chapter Fifteen: Solomon and Makeda's Reunion

From the base of the largest mountain we travelled across jungle and mountain, mountain and jungle even jungle covered mountains until we came to the Red Sea. We came to a large city nestled on the coast of the Red Sea. Standing on the shore you could faintly make out the land mass on the other side of the water. Solomon's grand Navy awaited his orders at this city. Makeda's General informed us we had to cross so we boarded Solomon's personal ship and crossed. Upon reaching the shores of the other side Makeda's General sent word that we had only a three days march to Makeda. Scouts dispatched to inform her of our arrival. Her land controlled the water access into the Red Sea. She had her own Navy guarding the entrance from the Indian Ocean.

We travelled for three days before reaching the grand castle of Makeda. Horns sounded upon our approach and the gates opened to the courtyard. We rode into the yard with the General and a few guards. Makeda stood in the middle of the yard next to Menelik who wore brown leather armor and a green cloak as the General had on. Makeda's General bowed before the Queen and announced our arrival. Solomon leapt from his horse walked to Makeda and gave her the most passionate kiss I had ever seen. She had seemed to get even more beautiful from the last time I laid eyes on her.

She smiled as Solomon held her and said, "My goodness love you seem as happy to be here as I am to have you." She bent around Solomon and said to me, "Moosie, it's been years and you've changed not. I hope you boys been keeping out of trouble?"

I unsaddled Falazel bowed and responded, "Yes my queen, as much as I can."

Solomon turned to Menelik who recently turned 14 and said, "Come over here to your father, and let me embrace you for the years I missed."

Menelik walked towards Solomon and said, "I tried to follow in your footsteps father. We must sit, talk and get to know each other better."

Menelik ran over and hugged me, "It is good to see you again Moosie, wise counselor of David and Solomon and he who does not age. I would like to sit a spell with you as well."

I nodded and said, "Sure Menelik, I am at your disposal."

Makeda interrupted all the formalities, "Come let us eat. A feast has been prepared, you must be hungry."

We sat at a large table and feasted upon chicken, fish, barbecued pig, nuts, berries, rice and wine. Solomon told stories of our trip. I ate until my stomach hurt. I had never tasted wine before and its effects sent me into a spin. I retired to my room thinking my mom would kill me if she knew I had been drinking at thirteen. I rationalized to myself in this country I am over fifty years old and had all the responsibilities of a counselor. That was my last coherent thought before I went into blackness. I awoke the next morning still in Makeda's kingdom with Solomon. We spent the next six months with Makeda and Menelik touring their large territory and listening to the expansion plans of Menelik. He loved architecture like his father and wanted temples and castles to be built all over the land.

Menelik and I became close because Solomon and Makeda spent many hours alone in chambers. During our time together he shared with me that he too had journeyed into the past and future as I am doing now. We sat in the courtyard on a hot clear day and stared out into the city.

Menelik turned to me and said, "I will hide the Ark for you."

I turned to him and replied, "Your father's Ark?"

He nodded and said, "Yes, I don't remember how I received it, but I am to keep it protected for you."

I touched my chest, "For Me?"

Menelik turned towards the city again and said, "We will meet each other again under different circumstances. I must first decipher my dreams to come up with some answers. Once my questions are answered I will be able to tell you more."

I too gazed back into the city to watch the coming and going of its people as I responded, "I understand Menelik, may you get the answers you seek."

On the fifth month into our visit with Makeda a scout came in for Solomon. He had word from Benaiah regarding the construction and also word from Nemrat. Construction of the vault had been completed and now awaited placement of the treasure. The scout also reported Nemrat had met with the new Pharaoh and served in the capacity of General of the troops defending Egypt from its Libyan threat. Solomon seemed happy to know Nemrat had not challenged the Pharaoh and waited for his fathers return. We spent one more month with Makeda. When the morning of our departure had finally come the guards waited to escort us to the docks. We planned to sail to the large mountain and unload Solomon's treasures into the vault.

Makeda with tears in her eyes asked Solomon, "Will you visit me again?"

Solomon grasped her hand with one hand and rubbed her ebony cheek with the other and replied, "My love you are but a sail away from me. The sea will carry me again to you."

Solomon bent over and passionately kissed Makeda's lips. He went over to Menelik and said, "Son, take care of your mother. Visit me when you can."

Menelik grabbed his fathers hand as he turned towards his mother and said, "Take me with you now; I will not be any burden."

Solomon turned to Makeda and said, "It is up to your mother. I would love for you to travel with me."

Makeda pointed at Solomon and smiled as she said, "Please take that boy with you! He wants an adventure with his father Solomon the King to tell everyone of."

Menelik smiled and said, "What is wrong with wanting to tour the World with Solomon the wise and his counselor?"

Makeda, Solomon and I all responded at the same time, "You are about to find out!"

We all laughed as Menelik ran to get his horse. He joined our party as we rode to the ships awaiting us at the sea. I turned for one last look at Makeda and waved at her as she disappeared into the distance.

Chapter Sixteen: El Arish

Upon reaching the ships we set sail from the Red sea through the Gulf of Aden and around the horn of Africa. We kept the coastline in sight as we navigated. We came to a point where we had land on both sides of us. We docked and went ashore to find out our exact location in relation to the stars. We landed not too far northwest of the construction site. We travelled about a month when in the distance we recognized the mountain shaped like a half moon. Benaiah wanted desperately to bury the treasure and return home. All told we had eighty ships packed to the rim with gold, jewels and other important items of Solomon's. We packed and sealed everything into the vault.

After closing the vault Solomon turned to me and said, "Moosie, remember this spot find your fortune on the mountain top when all else is taken."

I bowed and said, "Solomon I humbly thank you for your assistance and will work hard not to fail you."

Menelik said, "I do not recognize failure in you cousin, as I do not find failure in myself."

Solomon shook his head in agreement, "Our family does not take too kindly to failure. We are all working towards your success. May The Lord bless each of you."

As we all went to our separate tents a messenger came to Solomon with a private report. Whatever the report consisted of put Solomon in a horrible mood for a couple of days. As we packed up the campsite Solomon came to me and disclosed the contents of the report.

Solomon walked over to me and said with disappointment in his voice, "I have been informed what I feared to be is actually true."

I sat on a chair and asked, "What is true?"

Solomon went to a nearby tree and leaned back while looking up at its branches and said, "Mehetemwaskhe and Jeroboam are involved intimately. I left a spy behind to gather information and verify my suspicions."

I stood to my feet and said, "What are you going to do?"

He walked over to me with fire in his eyes and replied, "Catch them!"

He continued to walk past me towards Benaiah. He wanted everyone to be ready to leave by the following morning. General Benaiah went around hurrying everyone up to make sure by the time Solomon awoke the only thing left to do would be for him to get on his horse and ride. The next morning we set off towards the ships. We completed the journey back to the ships in fifteen days. We boarded the ships and Solomon gave the order for full sails and a hard row until we reached Eilat. He went below to his chambers for the next two days.

Menelik and I understood his rage, but no one ever saw him this furious before. Even Benaiah commented on Solomon's abruptness. He finally came out of his chambers and sat with Menelik and I. He seemed at peace until Menelik asked our destination upon reaching port.

Solomon turned to him and said, "We will visit El Arish."

Solomon stood up and walked away as he said, "We will make a ten days ride in four. I want to reach El Arish on the fourth night without word of my arrival and catch them in the middle of the night."

He slammed the door to his chambers and didn't come out again until we reached port. Upon reaching the shores of Eilat our horses were prepared with the necessary provisions. He gave the order for everyone to return to Jerusalem except for Menelik, Benaiah, a few guards and myself.

He turned to our tiny party and said, "We will ride hard and stop only to eat. We will open the gates to El Arish at midnight on the fourth day of our travel from this spot."

Benaiah grabbed Solomon's shoulder and said, "My lord what would you have me do if we catch them?"

Solomon removed Benaiah's hand from his shoulder and yelled, "I expect you to do your duty."

He jumped onto his horse and went into a full gallop towards El Arish. We all tore off after him into the darkness. Falazel surprised me with his speed. He easily caught Solomon and maintained his speed throughout the night. As we galloped through the never changing scenery of the open desert I thought of how jealous Solomon had seemed before we left and wondered what he would do if he caught Mehetemwaskhe in bed with Jeroboam. In four days time we reached the waters of the Mediterranean and only a few hours out from Arish. The full moon's position in the sky led me to believe it was close to midnight and from our speed we would arrive at our destination in about an hour.

In the distance the grand walls of El Arish casted a large shadow. Solomon's horse came to an abrupt halt. Solomon yelled for one of the few security detail we had brought along with us, "Go to the gates and have them opened. Tell them not to mention our arrival under penalty of death. I want my presence unheralded and concealed. Do you understand me?"

The guard shook his head and responded, "Yes my lord, I will return to you once the gates have been opened."

I began to get frightened because matters of the heart tended to make men crazy. I had never seen Solomon like this, and he reminded me of David and Joab before a battle. The specter of war had never been on Solomon until now. I dared not approach him. Whatever happened once we got inside the gates I would have to be with him lest he do something we all may regret in the morning. We waited for what seemed like an eternity for the guards return, in actuality only twenty minutes passed. He came back in a full gallop and reported.

He rode directly to Solomon and said, "My lord the gates are open and none have been warned of your arrival.

Solomon rode towards the gates of El Arish and said, "Moosie, come on. Everyone else stand fast."

As we came ever closer to the gate I became more nervous. I asked Solomon, "What are you going to do if you catch them?"

Solomon galloped faster and said, "Moosie, let us hope I don't."

We did not want anyone to notice the horses so we dismounted and walked towards the castle. The castle guard did not herald the king's entrance or speak. They opened the doors to the castle and lit the rooms as we entered them. We approached Mehetemwaskhe's chambers and the guard at the door touched his sword and put his finger to his mouth as to warn the king. Solomon and I drew our swords. We entered the chambers quietly and peaked from behind the foyer wall into the bedroom area.

What we witnessed put tears in my eyes and made me forget about Solomon for a moment. Mehetemwaskhe was naked and straddling Jeroboam with her hands on his chest. They had no covers on them so every detail of their love making sliced through Solomon's pride. The moment shattered when Solomon's cries of rage filled the chamber.

He had moved to the foot of the bed without being seen and said, "This is what happens when the King is away?"

At the sound of his voice Mehetemwaskhe rolled off of Jeroboam and immediately began to cry and apologize to Solomon. Jeroboam had turned deathly white as he got up from the bed and went for his sword and a pair of pants.

Mehetemwaskhe ran towards Solomon screaming, "No, don't hurt him!"

Solomon pushed her away and she fell back on the bed as Solomon responded, "Harlot, I will kill him and you should be more worried about your fate!"

Jeroboam had managed to put on his pants as he escaped Solomon's attempts to stab him. He grabbed his own sword and approached Solomon with his sword up and to the ready as he yelled, "Solomon, release her to me and we will leave peacefully. I love her and am willing to die if I cannot be with her."

Solomon raised his sword to defend against any strike and responded, "She is my wife and I am the king. Who do you pretend to be to make a deal with me for my wife?"

Mehetemwaskhe fell on the bed in a crumpled heap crying loudly for them both to stop. I don't think he noticed me or the guards in the room because Jeroboam moved forward to fight with Solomon. He lifted his sword to strike at Solomon when I came from behind the wall to assist with the fight. Jeroboam backed up as Solomon turned to me and put his hand up to halt me.

He said, "Moosie, this fight is mine and mine alone."

He lunged with a heavy overhead strike. Jeroboam moved to the right and blocked Solomon's swing. Solomon continued to advance and went for Jeroboam's head. Solomon's swordplay was good but Jeroboam seemed to be better. Jeroboam parried every thrust and countered with a swing of his own. I stood by hoping he would not get a lucky strike against Solomon and hurt him. Jeroboam swung wildly and Solomon partially blocked the swing with his arm knocking Jeroboam's sword to the ground. He took advantage of Jeroboam's not being armed and jumped on him connecting with several blows to his jaw.

They both fell back on the floor with Solomon landing on top of Jeroboam still swinging wildly. Jeroboam managed to get from under Solomon by hitting him with a hard shot to his ribs. As Solomon rolled off of him in pain Jeroboam got up grabbed his sword and jumped from the window. I ran towards Solomon to help him up and screamed for the guards to catch Jeroboam. Solomon and I got to the window in time to witness Jeroboam get up and run for his horse.

Solomon turned to the guards and said, "Bring him back here...dead or alive, it doesn't matter."

94

As they ran from the chambers I turned to him and said, "I will be in the guest chambers if you need me."

He looked at Mehetemwaskhe and said to me, "Moosie, I thank you for your help tonight. My wife and I have some talking to do."

I bowed before Solomon and Mehetemwaskhe before turning and leaving for the night. As I left Mehetemwaskhe still crying began to apologize to Solomon. I thought to myself how Solomon loved her and I knew he would not be mad for long and blame himself for her transgressions. I closed the doors tightly behind me for the night.

The next morning I arose and caught up with Solomon in the dining area. I walked in and asked him, "What happened after I left last night?"

Solomon popped a grape in his mouth and answered, "Jeroboam got away. He slipped into Egypt late in the night. I will get him, there is no place safe for him."

I asked, "What of Mehetemwaskhe?"

His stare did not leave the plate as he responded, "She will return to Jerusalem with us. We must find Jeroboam. I sent word to Nemrat of what happened and to have him search Egypt for the scoundrel."

I finished my breakfast and asked, "Are we staying here for a while?"

Solomon shook his head and said, "No, I cannot sleep in that bed. We leave as soon as all Mehetemwaskhe's clothes are packed and loaded. It has been a long journey since I have last slept in my bed back in Jerusalem. I want to get back as soon as possible."

I could tell something bothered Solomon but if he didn't want to talk about it I would wait for him to bring it up. I went to ready my horse for the long trip back to Jerusalem. My thoughts went to Jeroboam. Solomon now had a new enemy in a foreign land hiding like Absalom with David. He would not disappear quietly forever and by the expression on Solomon's face as he left the room I figured he had the same fears.

I woke up from my dream with Solomon sometime in the night lying on the hotel room floor where I fell asleep after praying. At first what seemed like a faint popping sound coming from the hall got extremely louder. It sounded like gunfire but I did not know for sure. The door had been dead bolted before I went to bed so I sat hoping nothing serious was about to happen.

After the morning conversation with Peter I had been a nervous wreck. Now with this going on I began to get even more nervous. I dialed down to the lobby to find out what the noise was but got no answer. I dialed once more and let the phone ring longer and still no one answered. As I placed the receiver back onto the hook the phone began to ring. I answered it slowly almost afraid of who it could be on the other end.

"Mustafa, lock the door and do not open it for anyone. Get far away from the door and hide behind something." The voice belonged to Peter but he sounded flustered and seemed to be on the move. I wondered to myself if I should even trust him at this moment.

"Peter, what is going on? Is that gunfire?" I said moving to the other side of the room away from the door. I grabbed the table and carried it with me to the corner of the room to use as a shield in case anyone tried shooting through the door.

Peter replied, "If anyone knocks do not open the door. In that case use the balcony and jump. We will secure the street below. You are only on the second floor so you will not be injured."

"You want me to jump from the balcony if there is a knock at the door?" I asked.

"That is exactly correct." He confirmed.

The phone clicked, Peter had hung up. I continued to hear the gunfire as it moved closer to my room. In the distance police sirens blared to let me know they were on their way to this mayhem. As I wondered how we were going to elude the police a loud explosion ripped through the room. The hotel shook as wood, smoke, glass and metal flew about. The table I grabbed kept me protected from the flying debris. Disoriented from the blast I realized I was being shaken by someone asking if I was ok.

"Yea, yea, I am alright." I said groggily as I slowly rose to my feet.

"Peter sent us to get you out of here. I am Judas. Put this on." The tall figure said.

I laughed and asked, "So Peter sent Judas for me, and I am supposed to trust you with my life with bullets flying everywhere?"

Judas laughed and responded, "I understand, but right now is definitely not the time or the place for this discussion. Either you can trust me and come with us or you can pull the bullets out of your ass when we leave. Please put this bullet proof vest on and the rest of this outfit before the police get here."

I chose to trust my Judas and quickly put on the black attire and bullet proof vest he had handed to me. He threw me a black helmet and a pistol. I checked to make sure there were rounds in the magazine and took the safety off.

He handed me a belt full of clips and said, "Stay close."

There were five men in the room including myself. We all wore black pants, black vests and black helmets with dark visors attached to them.

Judas turned to the rest of the team and said, "We're ready to move. Secure the hall."

He grabbed a radio from his hip and said, "We are moving to the roof. Prepare for extraction."

He whispered to me, "Shoot anything not wearing black."

I shook my head as I followed him from the room. We sprinted down the hall towards the exit sign. The team had cleared up to that point. We ran down the hall jumping over the scattered dead bodies. Some wearing black others wearing suits, blood stained the walls of the hotel. I tried not to focus on the carnage around me as I remembered the battlefield in Megiddo. I kept moving behind the team up the stairs. We ran up what must have been a million flights of stairs when finally we reached the roof. I did not notice anything peculiar. It was quiet, too quiet.

Judas turned to me and said, "Ok, the helicopter is not outside because the roof is not clear. We will have to clear this roof and we will need your help."

"Whatever I can do to help I will. Don't worry about me I will be ok." I replied.

He grabbed two grenades from his waste and opened the door to the roof slightly to toss them out. As soon as they exploded he opened the door wider and three of our men ran out on the roof. Automatic gunfire filled the roof as Judas and I left the staircase to find cover. We hid behind a stack of bricks piled on the roof left over from some project. I peeked from my position and counted four of the enemy shooting at us. The team had scattered across the roof so our shots rang out from many different spots which allowed me to peer out from my hiding spot and not be immediately targeted. I opened fire on a guy wearing a gray suit who shot at one of my team members to the right of me. I shot him three times in the chest. He fell to the ground dead.

The person standing next to him focused his aim on my position so I slid back behind my bricks as the bullets ricocheted around me. A chopper swooped in above us and an automatic whir of some kind of weapon filled the air. Hot brass fell from the chopper and burned my hands as it hit me. After two minutes only the sirens of the police who were now at the street level could be heard. The helicopter landed and we boarded. Judas was not with us for a second then appeared from the smoke carrying a body dressed in a suit. When he jumped aboard the helicopter we took off and immediately dropped very close to the water to avoid radar as we sped across the Mediterranean. I hadn't noticed before but I shook like a leaf from head to toe. All my experience before with warfare had been in the dreams. The fire fight tonight was very real.

Judas sensed my nervousness and said, "Mustafa it is over. You are safe now. Hopefully you will never have to hold a weapon again."

I nodded in agreement but somehow I knew that would not be the case. I didn't know anything about those protecting me. This made me feel a little uneasy but it would have to play out. So far I was still alive, this had to count for something.

Still not totally trusting my newfound friends I turned to Judas and screamed to be heard above the chopper engines, "Where are we going and why did you bring him?" I pointed to the wounded enemy gunman Judas had brought aboard the helicopter.

He screamed back, "We are going to our headquarters in El Arish. I brought him for an interrogation. I would like to find out what our enemies know about us." He smiled and returned his gaze back out over the water at the sun rising in the distance. We flew so close to the water it seemed I could reach out of the helicopter and grab a handful. I found it interesting that in real life I would soon be where I had last remembered King Solomon and I in my dreams. It couldn't have been a coincidence. I agreed that with all I had been through up to this point no such things as coincidences existed when dealing with the Lord. I sat back and closed my eyes. Thoughts ran through my mind of my dreams and of my current situation. Solomon had told me I would need the gifts he hid for me, but if I was dreaming would the gifts really be there?

I opened my eyes and spoke aloud, "Only one way to find out."

Judas turned to me and screamed, "What?"

I shook my head and replied, "Nothing."

Chapter Seventeen: Eden

I knew the treasures hidden by Solomon were necessary for me to do whatever the Lord had in mind for me to accomplish. I would use Peter and his organization to help me with the task of acquiring these treasures even though I did not fully trust them. They had saved my life, so I would give them the benefit of the doubt. I would discuss my plans with Peter when we arrived and hope he can be trusted. I looked around the Gunship at the four guys whom had pulled me from the roof of the Sheraton Moriah Hotel in Tel Aviv and wondered what experiences and unknown challenges awaited us?

We landed in El Arish and I didn't recognize the landscape. I had never actually been to Egypt, only in my dreams with Solomon but I somewhat expected Mehetemwaskhe's Palace walls to appear as the city came into view. We flew to a clearing where several vehicles and armed men gathered waiting for us to exit the chopper. I recognized Peter immediately and when the chopper landed I made a bee line straight towards him. I wanted answers and thought he might want the same from me.

"Peter, what happened?" I screamed trying to be heard over the whir of chopper blades.

He grabbed me gently by the arm and led me to a black Jeep. Once inside the Jeep he handed me a bottle of water and said, "Mustafa, things are becoming complicated. I will go over what we know once we are at base. I will need to know everything you do regarding your lineage."

I wondered what he meant by things are becoming complicated. I nodded as I thirstily guzzled the water trying to quench an unbearable thirst. My head spun as I came to grips with what I had experienced. I had tons of questions and wanted each one answered as soon as the opportunity presented itself. We drove for an hour deep into the desert. The extreme heat caused the air conditioner to work overtime to keep the Jeep cool. The Mountains and desert passed by the tinted windows. Sand and clay ruled the landscape while peaches grew everywhere. We drove up a winding mountain road until everything went black. We had driven underground, correction we had driven straight into a secret mountain side tunnel.

Peter unbuttoned his burgundy suit jacket and placed a tan colored hat on his head as he glanced over at me and said, "Welcome to base camp Mustafa. We call this place Eden. Someone will show you to your quarters. Clothes should be in the closet for you so you can shower before dinner. I will try to answer all your questions be prepared to answer many from us as well."

The Jeep stopped and Peter exited and walked briskly in the opposite direction from where I stood. A guard called out to me from across the parking lot. He had opened a door and signaled for me to follow him. I had no bags or clothes from home. Everything I owned had been left behind at the Moriah Hotel in Tel Aviv. I realized I had nothing. I guess I should be satisfied with still being in one piece. The guard led me through brightly lit corridors in a highly populated underground city. The guards pace slowed as he reached a doorway.

He turned towards me and said in horrible broken English, "We here, I come back twenty minutes."

"Thank you." I replied.

He smiled and walked down the corridor. I entered my room and the spacious apartment surprised me. The fully furnished space had a living room, dining room, kitchen, bathroom and a bedroom. Everything seemed perfect except for one thing. The home had no windows and bright lights hung from the ceiling instead. I went into the bedroom and fingered through some clothes hanging in my closet. I showered and dressed quickly. I wanted to be ready when the guard came back to escort me to my meeting. For the first time since all this started I wanted to take control instead of being controlled like a pawn.

When the guard returned I left the room in search of Peter and the answers he promised. We didn't walk too far when he stopped next to a room with large mahogany double doors. A board table with plush leather burgundy chairs sat in the center of the room. Large electronic screens with maps covered the walls and security cameras recorded the events in the room. A feast laid on the table as Peter, several men and a woman sat to eat when I arrived.

Peter greeted me, "Ah, Mustafa grab some food as I introduce everyone to you before we get started."

I quietly grabbed a seat next to Peter and prepared myself a giant plate of food as he walked over and stood next to a petite African American woman with glasses.

Peter introduced the young woman to me, "Mustafa this is Dr. Saundra Evans."

I smiled and nodded in her direction as Peter continued, "She is our chief Anthropologist and DNA Researcher. She will need some of your blood to run a few tests. Her code name is Mary."

He moved a few seats down to Judas, a rugged Arabic fellow who stood about 6'5 and always had a pair of shades on. Peter stood next to Judas and began to speak, "I am sure you remember Muhammad Zani, code named Judas. He is our tactical leader and weapons specialist."

I turned towards Judas as I bit into a piece of steak and smiled in appreciation of his services which to this point kept me alive. Peter moved on and stood next to a gentleman directly across from me at the table dressed in a white lab coat and squared dark brown glasses.

"Mustafa this is Dr. Leonard Hamilton our chief surgeon here at Eden." Peter said as he passed by the docs chair.

Dr. Hamilton interrupted Peter, "Hello Mustafa my code name is John. I will need you to come by my office for a physical as soon as you can."

I responded, "Glad to meet you John I can be by your office in the morning."

John shook his head in agreement as he answered, "Tomorrow morning will be fine."

Peter continued to move around the table. He now stood behind a gentleman dressed in a beautiful silk black and light blue pen striped three piece suit with a baby blue silk shirt and silk pink tie.

"Mustafa this gentleman is the Reverend Johnathan Frakes. He is our religious expert and also holds services here in Eden for its occupants. His code name is Matthew."

Peter moved to the last person seated in the room, "Mustafa, this gentleman will be able to assist in any historical confirmations or inquiries. Mr. Seth Kaufmann is a world renowned Historian and Archeologist. Code named Mark."

Peter sat down at the head of the large mahogany table and continued speaking, "You will meet the rest of our comrades later in the week. They are on their way here from various countries around the world." He took off his glasses to clean them. As he placed them back on his face he said, "I am Alan Jeffers. Currently I am charged with keeping you alive and to assist you in any way possible. We will now begin the meeting. We will attempt to fill you in on everything we know up to this point. Please feel free to ask any questions."

He turned to Mary and said, "Please start us off with the information you gathered?"

Mary stood and walked over to one of the screens on the wall. She reached for a remote on a ledge under the screen. When she clicked a button the screen lit up with the words "Cherokee Indian DNA Project" Mary then began to speak in a calm southern voice, "Some time ago it was discovered the Cherokee Indian shared some of the same practices in religion and customs with the Jewish faith. Scholars tried to identify how and where these two cultures met and merged. The Cherokee DNA Project was initiated publicly to search for a common link and geographical location.

Privately the project was initiated because the search for the heirs of Kings David and Solomon is still being conducted. Ever since the introduction of DNA research every skeleton or piece of bone taken from the earth is DNA sampled and catalogued."

"Most Americans are already in the DNA databank. Infants DNA are now being gathered right after birth. Every time blood work is done, standard practice is to send samples for DNA tracing. This way the government can paint an accurate picture of everyone's ancestry and ancestor's geographical footprint. Why they would want this information I still don't know yet. I do know when you had your physical your DNA was tagged as a match for being related to Kings David and Solomon. We had to verify and are still in the process of verification but someone else seems to want the chance to verify as well."

She moved back to her seat and sat down. As she sat she said, "Are you aware of any Cherokee stories or family members?"

I answered immediately, amazed at all the information starting to come together as we attempted to solve the mystery of me. "Yes, Cherokee blood flows through my veins. My mother's ancestors were Cherokee and my father's ancestors were Cherokee as well."

Dr. Evans smiled and said, "I would like to test if either of your parents ancestors were apart of the one percent true Jewish Cherokee population if I may."

Sitting in this room talking about the Cherokee nation sent my mind back to my time with Solomon when he was getting updated by his scouts regarding the progress of his pilgrimage expeditions. Sitting in the throne room at El Arish looking out over the calm Mediterranean I was listening to Solomon talking in the background to his security forces still hunting Jeroboam.

"Where did he hide in Egypt so fast? I want him in front of me now!" Solomon screamed at the top of his voice.

His Captain of security stepped forward and reported. "My King we have chased him past the Egyptian borders but were turned back by the

Egyptians. The new Pharaoh has given him refuge in the country and protects him. We will have to develop other means, a more covert method to capture him."

"Develop them! Inform Nemrat of our situation perhaps he can inform us of Jeroboam's whereabouts." Solomon said as he stood and walked towards the window where I sat.

The Captain replied, "Yes sir, we will dispatch a messenger at once." As he and his men exited the throne room.

No sooner had the security detail left when a chamber maid screamed from deep within the palace. The commotion was coming from Mehetemwaskhe's chambers. Solomon and I ran towards the screams with swords in hand expecting Jeroboam to be exacting some sort of revenge upon us. When we arrived at her chambers we witnessed a disheartening scene. Mehetemwaskhe was lying dead on the blood soaked bed.

There was a letter to Solomon on the floor near the bed apologizing for all the pain and embarrassment she may have caused to him. She explained how she could never forgive herself for cheating on Solomon and she prayed he could forgive her. Solomon dropped to his knees and cried aloud. Later, as I reflected I decided this was when Solomon changed. This incident and the betrayal of Jeroboam was the beginning of the nations decline.

Solomon was on his knees crying and then he ripped his shirt and screamed, "Why, Mehetemwaskhe. I loved you."

I went to him and helped him to his feet and said, "Solomon, come let's go. You don't need to be in here right now."

We walked slowly back to the throne room. Solomon seemed to be in shock. I sent for two messengers and several servants. Upon everyone's arrival I spoke to the servants first, "Prepare the queen's body for burial and the trip to Egypt. Please clean the chambers thoroughly." They immediately departed. I then turned to the first messenger and said, "Go to Pharaoh Psusennes and inform him of the queen's unfortunate death and our intentions to have her buried near her father."

"Yes sir, right away sir." The first messenger said as he left the throne room.

I then turned to the second messenger and said, "Inform Commander Nemrat of what happened here. Tell him also of our plans to transport the queen to Tanis for Burial."

The second messenger said, "Immediately sir." He then ran from the throne room.

I refocused my attentions on Solomon who was sitting on the throne with his head buried in his hands crying and murmuring to himself. He slowly lifted his head from his hands and said, "Moosie, I can't stay here anymore. Please prepare for our departure in the morning."

"Yes sir." I replied.

Solomon continued, "I also need for you to question the returning expedition scouts. You can inform me of what they tell you on the way back to Jerusalem."

As he stood and slowly walked from the throne room I replied, "Yes my king. I am truly sorry for your loss."

I sat by the window once more and waited for the first of the two returned expedition scouts to enter the throne room. As soon as he came in I began my questioning.

"Where did your expedition travel?" I turned to him and asked.

He handed me a drawing and took a minute to think before he responded, "Sir, we travelled West through the mouth to open waters."

I interrupted, "The mouth?"

I thought for a second and then realized he was talking about the straits of Gibraltar which many thought opened up like a mouth into the Atlantic Ocean. They travelled west to America, but in these times America had not been visited yet. Yet here was a scout telling me he had just returned from America with a drawing of the coast to prove it.

Anxious for the rest of his story I said to the scout, "Please continue, I am sorry."

He began his story from where I interrupted, "We travelled through the mouth to open waters. We then sailed Southwestward using the stars and sun until we came to the coast drawn there. We went down the coast and landed where I have placed the red X on the drawing."

I studied the drawing and the coastline appeared to be what I knew as Virginia and North Carolina. There was a large red X marked on the North Carolina coast.

He continued, "The X mark is where we left the ships and started to move inland. We moved westward from the X. Everything was green. The land there is bountiful until the coldness comes. We were not prepared for the cold white waters falling from the sky. We moved westward until it became warmer."

He handed me another drawing showing the route they used from North Carolina. It appeared they moved through Hickory North Carolina into Tennessee, Arkansas, Oklahoma, Texas and settled in what is now known as New Mexico. They travelled far from the coast searching for warmer climates. Studying the drawing a little closer I came to the impression they settled near Albuquerque. I turned to the scout excited because I actually recognized what he was trying to tell me and I understood he had just been farther than Columbus had ever travelled into the Americas.

I committed the map to memory then and said, "Thank you very much. That will be all."

The scout replied, "Sir, please inform Lord Solomon his items were placed at the settlement area and are now being protected."

I was bewildered at first then I remembered Solomon telling me he had left gifts for me at each location to be used in my time. I guessed these were the items in which the scout spoke of. The first man departed and held the door for the second scout as he entered the throne room. I sat down in my chair again ready for the tales of the second voyage.

I asked the young man, "Where did your journey take you?"

He handed me a drawing and began his tale, "We travelled westward with King Milesius' sons and Commander Nemrat. After passing through the mouth into open waters we sailed northwestward to a green coast. A storm came from the heavens and sent us from the coast for several days. Many died in the storm but our expedition faired well. After leaving our ships Milesius' troops went to war with the natives and came away victorious. Our expedition moved northwestward and settled where the X is marked on the drawing. Please inform Lord Solomon the items were placed in Torah Hill. Milesius' sons refer to the location as Tara Hill."

I went over the map carefully. The landing took place around Dublin and they travelled northwestward to what is known now as County Meath.

I thought this was getting interesting as I said to the scout, "You may leave. Thank you."

So far I had received the locations of two of the four expeditions sent out by Solomon. I would brief him on our long journey to Jerusalem. I arranged for our departure. Solomon was in no mood for conversation so I left him alone. It was during the next few months I began to notice a change in Solomon's behavior. He started becoming distant to me and would disappear with his wives for longer periods of time.

The next morning was cold and we left El Arish before the sun rose over the Mediterranean Ocean. We rode our horses hard and fast to Jerusalem and only stopped to sleep during the nights. My thoughts were interrupted by Mary's voice.

"Mustafa...Mustafa are you still paying attention?" She said as she was now standing over me shaking my arm.

I shook my head yes and asked, "Is there a map around?"

Peter got up from his chair and pressed a button on the remote. A screen with a map of the Earth's continents appeared. I walked over to the maps and remembered the first location being Albuquerque New Mexico.

"Peter, we need to visit Albuquerque. There is something buried near there." I said as I turned towards the table.

Peter scratched his chin and mumbled. Then he laughed and said, "Albuquerque, Los Lunas New Mexico. That's it!"

Mary hit her hand on the table as she said, "Yes, the Los Lunas stone!"

I was confused and asked, "What is Los Lunas and what does the stone have to do with us?"

Mary typed something into the computer and then put it up on the screen. A rock with writing on it appeared. She began to explain the picture, "There is a rock in Los Lunas New Mexico, right outside Albuquerque with the Ten Commandments carved in it."

"What does a rock have to do with our trip there?" I asked.

Mary stared at me like she couldn't believe I was asking such a stupid question, "The carvings are dated back to King Solomon's time. The writings are in ancient Hebrew."

I smiled and said, "This is where Solomon's first expedition finally settled. I trust this would be the same Jewish settlement who mixed with the Cherokee Nation. We must get to that stone. There is something buried there."

Peter returned to his seat and said, "Are there any other locations we should visit?"

I didn't think I should give them all the information I had right at this particular moment until I learned more about my gracious hosts, so I answered, "Let's just secure the stone first and then we can go from there."

Peter seemed to sense my apprehension and asked, "Mustafa, what questions do you have of us? I know this is a lot to take in at a moments notice."

I smiled and took him up on his offer. I sat down and said, "Peter, what is all of this and start from the beginning."

"I'll take this part." Mark said as he stood and walked to the front of the room. He sat on a small table and began talking, "The BIWF or British Israel World Federation as you know us today are the product of many smaller organizations merging to become what we are now. From day one our objective has been to protect all true heirs of King David and religious items from individuals and subversive organizations trying to put an end to our Christian/Jewish Constitution and Divine destiny. Throughout the centuries we have never had the opportunity to include people to our list. We have only protected items until we intercepted the cable."

"Your safety became our prime objective once it was confirmed you were the heir. Obviously it was none too soon after you barely escaped from Tel Aviv with your life. We covertly stopped Hitler from finding most of the relics he was after by finding them first or sabotaging his efforts. A few of our founders like the Reverend John Wilson and Richard Brothers have written books on our mission and our beliefs. We are here to keep you alive and assist you in any way you deem fit. If you are the sword we will try to sharpen your edge."

I sat back in my chair honored this organization had committed so much to my success and yet I felt I might let them down because I had no idea as of yet what my purpose was. I looked up at Mark and Peter and said, "I thank you for your help. I do not know my destiny or purpose but I know for sure I will move forward with you by my side as an ally."

Peter clapped his hands and said, "Magnificent! Your well being is our well being."

Matthew stood and said, "Before we leave this meeting let us bow our heads in prayer."

Everyone closed their eyes and bowed their heads as Matthew continued, "Lord, give us the strength to protect Mustafa from all evil attempting to befall him. Keep his enemies at bay. If for some reason Lord Mustafa should fall into the hands of the enemy deliver him safely from their grasp and back into our arms. Amen."

As everyone stood to leave Peter pulled me aside and whispered, "We have been picking up more radio traffic in the region than usual. I don't trust our security force would be ready for a large assault. If someone wants you bad enough they probably could muster a force to take you from us. Stop by the armory and pick up a weapon."

I asked, "Where do I go in case of an emergency?"

He whispered as to not cause any panic, "In cases of emergency we will be coming to you. Your guard will be tripled tonight but if anything should happen make your way to Hangar four."

I started to walk towards the door so I could get to the armory to pick my weapon when I noticed Judas walking directly towards me.

"Mustafa wait." He growled.

My feet planted in the marble at the sound of his grizzled voice. He reached out and handed me an earring.

"This has GPS tracking devices embedded in it so your location can always be tracked by us." He said.

I immediately put the earring in and said, "Thank you Judas, let's hope you never have to."

I turned and walked out of the conference room where my personal guard was waiting for me. It occurred to me I didn't know his name. I was trying to figure out what disciple I hadn't been introduced to yet so I could guess his name. I reached out my hand in a goodwill gesture and said, "My name is Mustafa. What is yours?"

He shook my hand and replied, "Sammie."

I laughed because I sure didn't expect a name like Sammie and asked, "Sammie can you take me to the Armory please?"

"Sure thing Mustafa, follow me." He said as he began walking briskly through the bright corridors.

His pace was unbearable. I could barely keep up as he twisted and turned around corner after corner. Every corridor was exactly like the one we had just gone through. The monotonous gray of the paint helped to confuse me further. Finally we stopped in front of an entrance with no doors. There was only a black curtain covering the doorway. Sammie stopped short of the curtain turned to me and nodded as if to say go ahead in. I walked slowly into a smoke filled room. There was a counter straight ahead of me with a large black bearded man watching a soccer match on a small TV hanging from the wall. He had on sunglasses and was smoking a cigar.

"What you want laddy?" He said with a cigar half hanging from his gray lips.

"I was told by Peter to come here for a weapon." I replied.

He stood from his bar stool and peered at me over the top of his sunglasses and said, "What ye be needin a weapon fer? You plan on gettin in some shootin?"

I felt nervous around this guy and my voice trembled as I answered, "No sir, I just needed it in case something happened."

He paused for a moment then laughed as he opened the door to the back and said, "Come on back son. I am Thomas O'Leary, but around these parts I go by Andrew. What kind a weapon do you be wantin?"

He shuffled through the door first and I followed. We entered a room as big as a football field with targets set up down range. There was a table with several weapons on it. The weapons had silencers on them and were loaded. There was a silver 9MM Beretta on the table, a pair of golden 9MM Glocks. There was also a suppressed M16 A2 rifle with a scope and an old out of place AK-47.

Andrew pointed to the table and said, "You know any of these weapons son?"

I thought to myself I am from Philly, but I said to him, "I have seen them before but I have never fired any of them."

He laughed and said, "Ah, that's your story and yer stickin to it eh."

We both laughed as he picked up the old AK-47 and handed it to me. "Try firin this baby. Be careful because it sprays bullets every which a way and the only method of correctly firin one of these puppies is short squeezes on the trigger."

I pointed the AK-47 down range and fired. BRRAAAPP, BRRRRAAAPPP, BBRRRRAAP. I turned back at Andrew and smiled.

He smiled back and said, "Oh how lovely she sounds when she be whisperin sweet nothins at me."

I handed him back the AK and asked for the M16 next.

Andrew gave me tips as I pointed the M16 down range, "Now with this baby you have to hold her tightly to ya. Squeeze the trigger don't pull it. You should be surprised when it goes off but you should be dead on target."

I fired the M16. Since it was suppressed only the sound of the rounds hitting the targets down range echoed through the room. Andrew was right I was dead on. This was my weapon.

I smiled and said, "I'll take it!"

He grabbed the weapon and wrote down the numbers engraved on the side of the it and said, "Good choice laddy. Here is plenty of Ammo and keep her on safe while walking in the corridors."

He handed the M16 back to me and continued to watch the soccer game I had so rudely interrupted. I ventured back through the black curtain to exit. Sammie was outside still waiting for me. I slung my weapon over my shoulder and said to Sammie, "Let's go back to the room. I am exhausted."

Sammie started walking his usual break neck pace through the corridors and it was all I could muster to keep up with him as we twisted and turned our way back to my room. When we returned to my room I went inside and hung my M16 in the closet by the front door. I guess I figured it would be safe from any harm in there. I was tired and tomorrow was going to be a long day with all the blood work and physicals they had prepared for me. It was hard to believe twenty four hours ago I was being shot at on a hotel roof in Israel.

I desperately needed sleep. As I faded into sleep I went back to my dreams with Solomon during a time when he was much older and becoming much more distant. Solomon and I sat together in his throne room not too long after our return from El Arish when we were visited by Commander Nemrat.

Nemrat walked proudly into the throne room and sat on the steps to the throne as he said, "Good morning father. How are you? Good morning Moosie extremely good to see you on this fine day."

Solomon glanced at me bewildered at Nemrat's unusually good mood as he asked, "No, the question is, how are you doing son? Your mother's death has caused me unbelievable pain and I can only imagine how it has affected you."

Nemrat hung his head as he said, "I have petitioned Psusennes to build a monument at Abydos. He is concerned because of her relationship with you and wants no foreigner to be memorialized in Egypt. The wording will be confusing because he also does not want Siamun to be named as well."

Solomon asked, "How can a person be memorialized with no mention of her father or husband?"

Nemrat replied, "He will use the name Siamun used before he became Pharaoh as father to Mehetemwaskhe and I don't believe there will be any mention of you as her husband. The entire Epitaph is confusing. I don't even know if I will be named as being her surviving son. Don't worry father when my reign comes I will right the wrongs."

Solomon stood and slowly exited the throne room as he said, "I have to leave you two for now. I have some religious affairs to attend to."

Nemrat looked over at me and said, "What is going on?"

I shrugged my shoulders as I answered, "Nemrat, your mothers death has made Solomon realize the importance of his wives in his life and he has chosen to spend more time with them."

Nemrat stood and walked towards my chair. He sat next to me and whispered, "Rumor is he allows matters of state to fall by the wayside and he is allowing his wives to practice their religions openly. He should be preparing Rehoboam for his rule. My brother is still too weak and easily influenced."

I tried changing the subject because Rehoboam was a sore subject around the kingdom. No one expected he could live up to his grandfather's or father's legacies. I leaned over to Nemrat and said, "Jeroboam is hiding in Egypt and your father has a bounty on his head."

Nemrat stood to leave and replied, "I have no ill will towards Jeroboam. He is a dear friend. My father and Jeroboam's battle is between them."

Sometime later Solomon and I sat down for what was to be our last conversation before his passing. Menelik had taken power and was now King of everything south of Egypt. Nemrat had risen to power and was now Pharaoh. Upon ascending the throne he changed his name to Shishak. Solomon was old and was preparing to leave the nation to Rehoboam but was apprehensive because of Rehoboam's lack of tactical and political experience.

Solomon stood from his throne, approached my chair at the table and said, "Mustafa, I am old and remember fondly our days together. My time on this earth is coming to an end. I pray the Lord forgives me for my transgressions. My sons rule from here to the tip of this continent, but I fear for Jerusalem after my passing. You must continue your presence here with us until the last two expedition scouts return with their reports. It is imperative you do not forget the locations of these settlements. If you are able please assist Rehoboam with anything he may need to keep Jerusalem intact as long as possible." His gaze then went out the window onto the beautiful city as the sun slowly set.

I waited awhile before I replied, "My King I will do all I can to guarantee Rehoboam's success. I have committed to memory the locations of the first two settlements."

Solomon leaned back in his chair and said, "A large battle awaits you in your time Moosie. I can only hope my father and I have shown you whatever it is The Lord wants you to learn from us so you can defeat the evil forces attempting take our precious Jerusalem from us."

I leaned close to Solomon and gripped his aged hand and said, "My time spent with you and David will never be forgotten. Even if this is somehow real, the times we have shared have been magical. I wish there was some way you could visit with me in my time to guide me."

Solomon laughed turned to me and placed his hand on my head and replied, "Moosie, this is exactly what we have done."

He stood up and started to walk towards the door. As he left he said, "I am so tired. I am going to take a nap."

Solomon never again rose. I cried for what seemed like days. The land was changing around me. The faces of the King's court changed. Rehoboam surrounded himself with young inexperienced counselors. Everyone came to say their last farewells to Solomon. His funeral procession stretched for miles. All of his sons Shishak, Menelik, Rehoboam and the others were present and paid their respects. Later as we sat in the throne room Shishak began to question the wisdom of Rehoboam surrounding himself with such young counsel.

"Brother, why are you older than all your counselors?" He asked Rehoboam.

Rehoboam replied sarcastically, "Nemrat, oh excuse me Shishak. My court is as much mine as your Egyptian court is yours. I don't question the age of your counselors."

Shishak glanced over at Menelik and I who were sitting at the table by the window gorging ourselves on some chicken and said, "Does not Mustafa's advice satisfy you?"

Rehoboam sat on his throne and replied, "Mustafa's time is yet to come. My time is now and I will be the greatest King Israel has ever seen."

Menelik and I almost choked on our food as Menelik said to Rehoboam, "Even better than David or Solomon? Brother even I can only hope to do half as much for my people as they have done here."

Rehoboam screamed back, "Then go and get started."

Menelik stood up fiercely and replied, "Brother be warned! Many enemies watch your borders and allies you will need in the near future. I will depart for home now."

Menelik hugged Shishak and I before he bowed to Rehoboam and left the throne room.

Shishak walked towards the throne and said, "Rehoboam, do not turn away those extending their hands to you."

Rehoboam now stood fiercely and said, "I don't need your help! Leave me, everyone leave me!"

Everyone left the throne room so the new King could be alone. He was hard on the people and from Egypt Jeroboam started gaining the love of the tribes. After several years it got so bad the country split in two. Jeroboam leading one half and Rehoboam still based in Jerusalem leading the other. Civil war was inevitable. A scout arrived from Shishak and quietly knocked on my door.

"Lord Mustafa, Pharaoh Shishak asks if his father's treasures are safe. Most importantly is the Ark safe?" The scout asked as he entered my room.

I sat on my bed and replied full of sorrow, "Inform Pharaoh they may not be for long."

As quickly as the scout appeared he disappeared with the news. Several months passed until one morning I was awakened by a tremendous horn blast. One Jerusalem has not heard since the first night of my dream when we seized Jerusalem for David. I quickly arose from bed and went to find out what the commotion was. When I got outside I was greeted by a site I hadn't seen in years. Standing before me was Shishak, Menelik and their hosts of armies.

They both got off their horses and walked towards me. We hugged and Shishak said, "Let us take this into the throne room."

Once inside we met with Rehoboam who was beside himself with fear and anger.

"What in the hell is this Shishak?" screamed Rehoboam.

"I am here to peacefully gather father's treasures and take them to where they can be properly protected." replied Shishak.

Menelik stepped forward and said, "I shall assist with the protection as well."

"You are here in a peaceful manner yet everything around you is war." Rehoboam said walking towards Shishak. "You assume I would let you take my treasures." He was now face to face with Shishak.

Shishak grimaced and said, "I am father's oldest son and these treasures are more mine than they are yours. You are about to be overcome by your enemies and you would try to deny me the privilege of protecting my father's treasures."

Shishak was furious; he grabbed Rehoboam by the throat and almost lifted him off the ground. Rehoboam's guards tried to intervene but Menelik and I drew our swords and blocked their paths. They immediately backed away.

Shishak then told him, "Nothing will stop me from protecting my father's treasures and making sure they make it to their final destinations. Your borders are unprotected no one even thought to challenge my forces as we came all the way to Jerusalem."

He let Rehoboam go and watched as he fell to the ground on his knees.

Shishak finished, "I am taking the treasures of Jerusalem and going to all the major cities of Israel and gathering the treasures of those cities as well. This land is cursed until it can be restored by an heir who can reunite and protect the treasures."

Rehoboam crawled to the throne and said, "Do as you wish brothers, my end will not be as soon as you think." He then got up and walked out.

Menelik turned to me and said, "Mustafa I will place the Ark with the other treasures in the first burial site on the mountain top."

I shook my head and replied, "Thank you Menelik. May your travels be peaceful. I will stay here for as long as possible.

Shishak grabbed my arm and said, "When your time is done here please visit my court. You are welcome anytime."

He then gave the order to his military commanders for everything on the lists to be gathered. The process of gathering all the items took about a month and I enjoyed the time I spent with Menelik and Shishak.

BOOOM!

My dreams were shattered by the earth shaking. I grabbed my bed as to not fall out of it. I leapt to my feet and ran towards the closet to get my M16. Several explosions ripped through the tunnels. As I reached for the closet door and explosion blew me back away from the closet door and across the room onto the couch. My head was spinning and the room was filled with smoke. In the distance someone was speaking what I believed to be German. I slowly rose to my feet still feeling light headed.

When I reached the blasted doorway someone stuck a weapon in my neck and said in a deeply accented voice, "Please give me a reason…Mustafa." I put my hands up just in time to feel the heat and jolt of electricity running through my body as I was tazed. I remembered hearing horrible laughter as everything went black around me.

Breinigsville, PA USA
21 March 2011
258093BV00001B/28/P